Book # 2

D0935132

Dear Reader,

The relationship between sisters can be a strong force in the sisters' lives. That's certainly been the case in my life, and it's the case for Betty and Mary.

My sister and I are only fifteen months apart, and when we were growing up this often led to competition. Over time we learned to shed the competition and embrace our friendship. Today she's one of my best friends, much as Betty is for Mary.

Maybe your relationship with your sister (or other family member) has never matured past childhood competitions. My prayer is that as you read this story, the strength of relationship between Mary and Betty would encourage you. It is possible to have a wonderful relationship with a sister (or mother, brother, or father). Sometimes it takes a lot of prayer. Other times it takes a willingness to confront in love. Always it requires a belief that it is a relationship worth the fight. Ultimately, it is a love that can transcend all types of strain and challenge.

This book is also a story of community and how the people in our lives come together when we most need them. Mary is humbled by the way people continue to express their love for Mary and Betty. In those times of trial, I am so grateful for the people God has brought into my life. I pray you have that same sense of extended community in your lives.

I hope you enjoy this trip back to Ivy Bay.

With love,
Cara Putman

Secrets of Mary's Bookshop

SECRETS of MARY'S BOOKSHOP

MIXED MOTIVES

Cara Putman

Guideposts

New York

Secrets of Mary's Bookshop is a trademark of Guideposts.

Published by Guideposts Books & Inspirational Media
110 William Street
New York, New York 10038
Guideposts.org

Acknowledgments

Every attempt has been made to credit the sources of copyrighted material used in this book. If any such acknowledgment has been inadvertently omitted or miscredited, receipt of such information would be appreciated.

"From the Guideposts Archives" originally appeared in *Daily Guideposts 1993*. Copyright © 1992 by Guideposts. All rights reserved.

Cover and interior design by Müllerhaus
Cover illustration by Ross Jones, represented by Deborah Wolfe, Ltd.
Typeset by Aptara, Inc.

Printed and bound in the United States of America
10 9 8 7 6 5 4 3 2 1

MIXED MOTIVES

ONE

⬥◆⬥

Mary plucked her purse from one of the cubbies beneath the marble-topped display counter in her store, Mary's Mystery Bookshop. She'd taken a few extra minutes after the long workday to clean up the now quiet aisles. Then she'd shelved a new shipment of paperback mysteries. These titles were perfect for readers who visited Cape Cod and wanted engaging stories that could fill a few hours while they relaxed either on Ivy Bay's beaches or in cabins.

While the current dreary spring days weren't warm enough to entice many to the beach, Mary knew it wouldn't be too many more weeks before these books flew off the shelves and out the door in the hands of happy customers. Oh, she loved that process of matching the right mystery with a customer.

With that thought, she grabbed the stack of new catalogs to look at later that evening. It wouldn't hurt to start planning her summer promotions now.

Mary couldn't wait until the sun broke through and everyone could celebrate springtime. That hope had been central in Mary's mind as she created this month's recipe for Bailey's Ice Cream Shop. In honor of Saint Patrick's Day, she'd created Shamrock Pot of Gold, a blend of green mint ice cream with walnuts and pineapple chunks. The unique blend had come together as she aimed for the green of a shamrock. And the warmth of the spring sun would feel like a pot of gold, so she'd added pineapple plus a few walnuts for crunch. After a couple of tries, the blend was perfect, and she couldn't wait to see what the Baileys thought.

After she checked her purse to make sure the ice-cream recipe card was still tucked in the side pocket, she glanced around her shop, a smile tugging her lips. She'd been blessed with beauty from ashes when her beloved husband, John, passed away. In the days after his death, she'd wondered if she could turn her dream of opening a mystery bookshop into reality. Now she stood in her store and felt his benediction.

Her life was good.

Ivy Bay fit her every bit as well as Boston, even though the two were so different. Here, she was part of a tight-knit community that expanded beyond her church and work. It was hard to go anywhere without being greeted by at least one person. She was blessed to be doing what she loved in this place that, as a child, she had visited most summers.

The best part was spending so much time with her sister, whom she'd moved in with after relocating to Ivy Bay. Betty hadn't called all afternoon, which was unusual but not a cause for concern. They both led full lives—Betty enjoyed community projects and gardening as much as Mary loved her bookstore and piecing together the clues of an occasional mystery.

After locking the door behind her, Mary crossed Main Street and then walked up the block to Bailey's Ice Cream

Shop. The vintage ice-cream parlor had bubblegum-pink-and-white-striped wallpaper, matching pink padded stools, and large display coolers filled with ice cream made by the Baileys. Paige Bailey stood behind the counter, a forest-green ribbon tucked like a headband through her dark pixie-cut hair.

"Hi, Mrs. Fisher. Can I get you anything?"

"Not tonight, Paige. I just stopped by to drop off the recipe for my new ice-cream flavor." She dug out the recipe card and handed it to Paige. "See what you think of this one."

Paige's mouth moved as she silently read the ingredients. "I wouldn't have thought to mix the green mint with walnuts and pineapple, but I bet it will be good." She looked up at Mary with a twinkle in her eyes. "Thanks so much, Mrs. Fisher. Mom will probably mix up a test batch tomorrow. Be sure to swing by after work."

"See you then."

The brisk air kept Mary moving as she headed back to the shop for Gus, her cat. She put him in his carrier, then walked home. She tried to stay ahead of the chill that sought to penetrate her lined mackinaw. When she turned the knob on the front door of the Federal-style home she shared with Betty, she found it locked. Maybe Betty wasn't home yet, though Mary couldn't remember her sister mentioning an evening outing. Gus's plaintive meow communicated he was as ready to get out of his carrier as she was to get inside. She set his carrier down and dug out her keys. As soon as she unlocked the front door and released him, he strutted down the hall before coming back to twine around her legs with a loud purr.

"Betty? I'm home." Silence greeted Mary as she shrugged out of her coat and hung it on the coat tree. Maybe her sister had headed out for dinner. If so, Betty had probably left a note in the kitchen.

After changing into lounge clothes, Mary headed to the kitchen. She glanced at the fridge and countertops for a note but didn't see one. Well, Betty would surely be home soon.

Mary fixed a sandwich while tomato soup heated on the stove. After pouring the soup into a bowl, Mary added some croutons and sat at the kitchen table with her meal. The house felt quiet without Betty, but Mary appreciated the added layer of peace that wrapped around her after her hectic day. Her shoulders unknotted, and she let her thoughts wander as she flipped through one of the catalogs she'd brought home from the shop.

As soon as she cleaned up supper and returned the catalog—now flagged with Post-it notes—to her purse, she headed upstairs to her bedroom and claimed the latest Randy Singer legal thriller from her bedside table.

Book in hand, she returned to the living room. She'd read down here while she waited for Betty. She curled up on the blue-and-white-striped damask sofa, and Gus hopped onto the cushion next to her. He fixed his gaze on her. It was only when she stroked his back that he curled up next to her and cleaned his paws.

Time flew as she turned the pages in the book. After a while, she got thirsty and headed to the kitchen to fix a mug of tea. When she turned on the burner under the teakettle, she glanced at the stove clock and paused.

Could it really be nine o'clock?

Betty usually made it home before now, and if she didn't, she'd call to let Mary know when she anticipated being home. It wasn't something she needed to do, but it was a courtesy the two had adopted shortly after Mary moved in.

Mary glanced at the phone on the counter, then back at the clock. Betty was an adult and didn't need Mary worrying needlessly about her. If Mary called, she'd embarrass or annoy her sister. She tapped her fingers on the countertop as the kettle whistled. There was no harm in waiting a while longer. If Betty didn't arrive in the next half hour, then Mary would call Betty's cell phone before heading to bed.

Gus shifted as she sat on the couch, a reproachful glint in his eyes as he sniffed.

"You're fine, Gus."

He turned away from her, and she picked up her book. The plot that had pulled her through the chapters now competed with her concern for Betty. Before the half hour had passed, she pulled her cell phone from her purse and dialed Betty's number.

The call immediately clicked over to voice mail. "Hey, Bets," Mary said. "Hope your day's gone well. Just checking in. Call me when you can."

Mary ended the call, then tapped the phone against her chin. Why had it gone straight to voice mail? Perhaps Betty's battery had died. Or maybe she had simply turned it off for a while. In all likelihood, Betty was enjoying a nice evening with friends and would have an array of stories to share when she returned home. Maybe they'd gone to a movie and Betty had turned off the phone so it wouldn't disturb anyone.

Betty could certainly take care of herself and would call if she needed anything.

"Let's go to bed," Mary said to Gus, though part of her didn't like the thought of doing so before she knew Betty was home. Mary tried calling again but still didn't get an answer.

Well, there really wasn't anything she could do to locate her sister. Not now. She had to trust that Betty was fine, and they'd share a laugh about Mary's concern in the morning.

Mary went through her nightly routine. Gus walked in and out of her bathroom as if he couldn't settle down either. It just wasn't typical for Betty to be out this late without letting Mary know.

"Gus, we can't worry about her."

But that didn't stop the unsettled feeling from following Mary as she went back downstairs for a glass of water. The house phone rang as she turned off the light in the kitchen.

Mary set the glass on the counter, and the water sloshed over the sides. She answered the phone.

"Mary? Thank goodness! This is Eleanor."

"Is everything all right?"

Eleanor Blakely, Betty's sister-in-law, sounded oddly out of breath for this time of night. She usually portrayed the perfect image of a New England woman with wealthy roots. She practically dared the wind to touch her perfectly coiffed hair.

"I don't know. I don't think so." Eleanor took a stuttered breath. "Is Betty there?"

"No. I'm sorry, but I haven't seen her all day. I'm not sure where she is."

"Of course she isn't there. I wasn't thinking. But it can't be true." Dread laced Eleanor's normally modulated voice. Mary could picture her covering her mouth with one hand,

and the unsettled feeling Mary had ignored all night clamped its claws into her.

"Eleanor, what's going on?"

"I think you need to come over, right now. I've had a terrible call. The police are on their way."

"Of course I'll come over. What happened?"

"It's about Betty. She's been kidnapped."

TWO

◆◆◆

Mary stared at the phone after Eleanor hung up abruptly, then hurried upstairs and threw on a fresh pair of jeans and a turtleneck. She scooped up her cell phone from its charger and grabbed her purse and coat. She hurried from the house and down the sidewalk to her car. Her fingers trembled as she slid the key into the ignition of her sedan.

Eleanor's call scared Mary, and her mind scrambled into a dizzying maze of questions. What should she do? She pulled to the side of the road and called Pastor Miles. Even though it was late and she didn't know much, she knew he would pray. Mary needed to know someone was assailing heaven on Betty's behalf while she went to Eleanor's for answers.

After he answered, Pastor Miles listened to her rushed words that sounded crazy. "Kidnapped? What? How? I don't...Of course I'll pray. Keep me posted."

"I will. Thank you. I'll call back as soon as I know something."

Then Mary dialed her friend Henry Woodrow as quickly as her trembling fingers allowed.

"Hello?" His voice sounded as alert as if it was the middle of the day, though Mary knew she could have woken him from sleep if he had an early fishing expedition planned in the morning.

"This is Mary. I'm so sorry to bother you."

"Never a bother. What's going on?"

"I'm not sure." She relayed Eleanor's cryptic call. "Could you pray for Betty?"

"And for you. Is there anything I can do?"

"Not until I know more. I'll call after I talk to Eleanor."

"You're headed there?"

"I'm a couple of blocks away."

There was a moment of silence, then a muffled sound as if Henry's whiskers brushed the speaker. "Keep me posted."

"I will." Mary dropped the phone in her purse, pulled back onto the road, and then turned on the street that led to Eleanor's home.

A few minutes later, she parked in front of the elegant gray house. Normally, Mary might appreciate the beautiful home and landscaping, but tonight all she could think about was getting inside and finding out what was going on.

A police car pulled to the curb in front of her, lights and sirens off. Chief Benjamin McArthur stepped from the vehicle, and a moment later, a second car pulled up. This one was driven by Deputy Bobby Wadell. Seeing them made Eleanor's crazy claim, that Betty might have been kidnapped, seem possible. But how could it be?

Mary pulled out her phone and tried Betty's cell one more time. Eleanor's impression could be wrong. Surely Betty hadn't been kidnapped, and if she could get her sister on the phone, Mary could prove it and clear up the whole mistake. But as the call went straight to voice mail again, Mary slumped against the seat.

Something was definitely wrong.

The two police officers waited on the sidewalk, looking at her car. Chief McArthur and Deputy Wadell were good at their jobs. A big man, Chief McArthur cared deeply for the people of his town. If Betty was really missing, they'd find her. She had to believe that. Chief McArthur patted Wadell on the back, then headed toward her. Time to get out if she didn't want the chief to see how fear had clamped into her. She opened her door and stepped out of the car. As much as she wanted to deny she needed to be here, she couldn't leave. Not until she knew everything she could learn about what was happening.

Chief McArthur stopped in front of her. "Hello, Mary. Where's Betty?"

"I don't know." Those three words emphasized how little she could help. She didn't have any idea where Betty was or how she'd spent her day.

He towered over her in his uniform as he guided her up the sidewalk. It didn't matter that it was approaching 10:00 PM—his uniform looked pressed and fresh, and his voice was as kind as if she were the first person he'd dealt with all day. "When did you last talk to her?"

"This morning. We shared a cup of coffee before I went into the store."

"Did she mention any plans?"

"None. And I didn't notice anything on her calendar either." Betty hadn't mentioned anything at breakfast;

Mary was positive. When she left for the bookstore that morning, it had seemed like any other Tuesday. Nothing had suggested Betty would disappear. "Do you think she'll be okay?"

Chief McArthur stopped her as they reached the door. "We'll find her, Mary. I'll dedicate all the resources I can to finding her."

"Thank you." Mary tried to smile, but her face wouldn't cooperate. "Why does Eleanor think Betty was kidnapped?"

"Betty called and told her."

Mary stared at Chief McArthur. Eleanor hadn't mentioned that in her crazy call. And it just didn't fit. Other people might treat a call like that as a bad joke, but Betty was too kind and considerate. She preferred a sweet story to a hard-core detective novel, because life was scary enough.

"Betty called Eleanor and told her she'd been kidnapped?"

"Yes, though I'll learn more when we get inside. You're sure Betty didn't mention anything? Any place she was going? People she planned to see?"

"No, I left during breakfast, while she was reading the *Bugle*. Everything seemed normal." Like every other day.

The door opened before Chief McArthur knocked, as if Eleanor had waited by the window for their arrival.

"Thank goodness you're here, Chief. Hello, Mary." Eleanor still looked as elegant as always, but there was a wild look in her eyes. Something Mary had rarely seen in Eleanor's usual supercomposed persona. "Betty's call was the strangest thing. I wasn't prepared for her words. And then a man came on, claiming to be her kidnapper." Eleanor shuddered as she stepped back from the door.

They filed into the hallway, and Chief McArthur studied Eleanor. "Are you sure that's what you heard?" His voice was gentle even as his gaze searched her face.

Eleanor shifted her body in front of a table topped by a gilded mirror. "I know it sounds crazy, so crazy I almost didn't call. But Betty did call me to tell me she'd been kidnapped." She wrapped her arms around her middle and then nodded toward the living room. "And as I said, she wasn't the only one on the call." Eleanor looked around as if not seeing her own home. Then, slowly, she shook her head and glanced at Mary. "Let's go in the living room while I explain."

Once everyone was settled, Chief McArthur pulled out his slim notebook and focused his attention on Eleanor. "Tell us everything that happened."

"It was about nine thirty when my phone rang. I was surprised when I recognized Betty's voice." Eleanor leaned forward, arms still wrapped tightly around her stomach. "She and I talk often, but never at that hour. At first, I was concerned something had happened." She paused and her eyes became shadowed. "I just never expected what she said."

"And that was?" The chief was more patient with Eleanor than Mary would have been. She needed to know immediately every word her sister had said.

"It was so simple I wrote it down." Eleanor stood and walked to the antique phone table. She grabbed a piece of paper and handed it to the chief.

He scanned the paper. "You're sure that's all she said?"

"Yes." Eleanor stared at the sheet as if reading its words from a distance. "After I called you and Mary, I began to write it down. I've tried to remember everything she said. She didn't even sound distraught. It was so odd."

The chief studied the paper for a minute. Then he pointed at something. "What does this mean?"

Eleanor looked at the paper. "I was getting ready to write down the rest when you arrived." She took a deep breath. "After Betty finished, there were a few seconds of static. I thought the call had ended but didn't dare hang up until I was certain. Then a man spoke."

"What did he say?" The chief's voice remained calm, though he leaned forward farther.

"That I'd get a ransom demand tomorrow morning. I was to start working with my bank so money would be ready when he called."

"Did he state a specific ransom demand?" Deputy Wadell's voice matched the intensity of the chief's body position.

"No. And I thought that was strange. He simply said he'd call again."

Deputy Wadell looked at Chief McArthur. "Why not just say what he wants now?"

The chief shook his head. "I don't know." He turned back to Eleanor. "Did you recognize his voice?"

The question lingered in the air. Mary prayed that Eleanor would answer in the affirmative. They needed a way to find Betty and free her from whoever held her.

Eleanor fidgeted with her hands. "No. His voice was strangely deep, like he was forcing it to sound different. And he wasn't on the phone long. Just enough to say those few words." She looked at Mary, anguish in her eyes. "I'm so sorry, Mary. I should have done more."

Mary reached across the space and patted Eleanor's knee. "I'm sure you were shocked."

"I was. But it still feels like I should have done something."

"Bobby, let's get a call into Boston." Chief McArthur stood. "We'll need their assistance on this."

Deputy Wadell nodded and got to his feet. He pulled his cell phone from his pocket before he left the room. A moment later, Mary noted the soft sound of the front door opening and closing.

A shiver swept up her spine, and she wrapped her arms around her middle, a part of her mind recognizing she now mirrored Eleanor.

"What are we going to do, Chief?" Eleanor's voice held a note of desperation. "Why would she call me if she was kidnapped?" Eleanor turned to Mary and said, "Wouldn't she have called you?"

Mary was asking herself the same question.

"Well, Eleanor, if there's a ransom, you are in a better position to pay, though I hate to state it so bluntly." Chief McArthur glanced at his notes.

"Did Betty feel okay when you saw her this morning, Mary?"

"She seemed to. She didn't say anything." But Betty wasn't the type to complain. If she did, it was because her rheumatoid arthritis had placed its vise on her. Her sister had moved easily that morning and hadn't grabbed painkillers with her coffee. "No, I'm certain she felt fine."

"That's good." The lines around Chief McArthur's eyes didn't match the sure tone of his words. "Definitely better than if we had to worry about her having some kind of attack and wandering off."

"I'm as certain as I can be that didn't happen. Betty would have stopped and called for help." The chief looked at her, and Mary realized he meant she might not be able to call for help.

Mary pointed at the note. "May I see it?"

The chief held on to the paper for a couple more seconds as he reread it, then handed it to Mary.

Mary tried to still the paper in her trembling fingers.

Hello, Eleanor. I'm okay, but someone has kidnapped me and he wants to talk to you. Tell Mary that for now I'm oka—

The words squiggled to a stop as if Eleanor had been interrupted by their arrival. Betty's words were certainly matter-of-fact, even though they held a veiled threat.

The doorbell rang, and a moment later, the door opened. "Aunt Eleanor?"

Mary stood as her nephew Evan Emerson walked into the living room.

"Aunt Mary? You're here too?" Evan stood in the doorway, his shoulders slumped. "I hoped Aunt Eleanor was wrong." He took in the chief. "Guess not."

Chief McArthur stood. "We'll do all we can to find your mother, Evan."

Evan walked to Eleanor, and after she stood, he gave her a quick hug. Then he turned toward Mary and collapsed onto the sofa next to her.

She hugged her nephew, then reread the words on the note before turning to Eleanor. "Is this all Betty said?"

Eleanor reached for the note, yet didn't look at it. "Betty did say the oddest thing. I was about to write it down when you arrived. It was so odd I almost asked her to clarify, but that man came on the call." Eleanor handed the note back to Mary. "She said, 'Hang ten, Eleanor.' Can you imagine?"

"Hang ten?" Evan snorted and pushed to his feet. "That's not the kind of phrase my mother would say."

Mary agreed with Evan. She tried to imagine why Betty would use such a phrase in the midst of an incredibly tense situation.

"The other thing that was odd was that she said it after a pause," Eleanor added. "As if she had to think." Eleanor rubbed her arms. "It didn't make sense at the time and still doesn't."

Chief McArthur took the note from Mary and then jotted the words on Eleanor's call transcript. "Does it mean anything to you, Mary?"

She thought another minute, then shook her head. "Can you understand why she would have said that, Evan?"

"Not at all." He looked completely befuddled. "I've never heard Mom say the phrase, not even after watching *Teen Beach Movie* with Betsy and Allison. But there's a lot about this day I don't understand."

Mary turned to Chief McArthur. "Could it be something the kidnapper made her say?"

"I suppose. It does seem highly unlikely that would be a phrase she would use. Especially in a tense situation like this." He turned to Eleanor. "And right after that, the man got on the phone?"

Deputy Wadell returned to the room, his face slightly taut as he moved toward the chief. He leaned down and whispered in the chief's ear and then walked into the dining room.

"Sounds like the equipment we need is on the way from the Boston PD." The chief rubbed a hand over his face. "We've never needed anything like this before. According to Bobby, Boston is sending a tech with the equipment. She should arrive within the hour."

That should have made Mary feel better. Chief McArthur was treating this as a real threat. He'd already put things in motion with a larger police department, something that couldn't have been easy. Yet it felt insignificant. She needed to be out doing something, looking somewhere.

The deputy looked at Mary. "What phrase were you talking about when I returned?"

"Betty told Eleanor to hang ten at the end of the call."

Deputy Wadell's face wrinkled as he thought. "That doesn't sound like Mrs. Emerson."

Mary nodded. "Exactly." She just couldn't picture those words flowing from Betty. "Did she say them any certain way?"

"I'm not sure what you mean." Eleanor studied her hands. "But they seemed abrupt. Almost as if the kidnapper snatched the phone out of her hands."

A chill went up Mary's spine as the chief made a notation, then looked at Deputy Wadell. "Why don't you head back to the station and do a quick search on the phrase? See if anything pops up locally related to 'hang ten.'"

"I'd like to wait until the tech arrives, if you don't mind. The Boston PD agreed to send someone with the equipment we'll need, but it's going to take a while for the officer to arrive."

Why wouldn't Deputy Wadell hurry off to do what the chief asked? Mary didn't like that he was delaying on the only realistic lead they had. Slim as it was, it was all they had at the moment.

Chief McArthur frowned at his deputy. "There's no need for you to wait."

"I'd like to know how to set up and work the equipment, in case she has to leave."

It sounded reasonable, but couldn't Chief McArthur do that?

"All right. But as soon as it's all set up, I want you back at the station."

"Yes, sir." Deputy Wadell pulled out his smartphone. "I'll try a preliminary search on 'hang ten' from here."

Mary rubbed her temples, feeling her pulse surge through them with each beat of her heart. Maybe the building pain explained why she couldn't understand what had happened. Everything seemed so confusing since the call. And so much seemed out of place, out of order. Betty calling. Betty using that odd phrase. Mary shook her head, trying to find clarity but failing. "This doesn't make any sense, Chief. Why would Betty make the call? Doesn't the kidnapper usually do that?"

The tall man shrugged, keeping a close eye on her. "I don't know. We don't have many kidnappings around here. Maybe he wanted Eleanor to know Betty is okay so that she would have incentive to fulfill his ransom demand."

Mary thought another moment. "But Betty is the last person someone would kidnap."

Chief McArthur's expression firmed, as if he were about to ask a hard question. Mary braced herself for whatever it was. "I hate to ask, Mary, but...is anyone upset with Betty that you know of?"

Mary understood why he needed to ask the question, but she couldn't think of a single soul who was angry with Betty—especially not anyone who would take it to this degree. She shook her head as the soft tap of Deputy Wadell's fingers on his phone formed background noise.

"All right. That's about what I expected. Eleanor…" The chief and Eleanor leaned toward each other and murmured something, yet Mary felt caught in an eddy of words. They swirled around her, but she couldn't understand them.

Where was her sister? Who had taken her? Why not leave the ransom demand now? What did the kidnapper have planned? The questions raced through Mary's mind followed by a tightening in her shoulders. Could Betty really be okay, or had she been forced to assure Eleanor?

Fighting down the panic that threatened to overwhelm her, Mary turned to the chief. "Are you set up for Eleanor to receive a ransom demand, in terms of tracing the call and tracking devices?"

"Not yet, but Boston PD will handle that as soon as possible."

Evan sighed and shuddered. "Are we really talking about tracing phone calls from someone who kidnapped my mother?" His voice rose with each word.

Chief McArthur nodded, his attention focused tightly on the younger man.

Evan turned toward Mary. "Aunt Mary, what will we do?"

"Search for her." Tears welled in Mary's eyes.

Evan slid closer on the couch and gave her a quick hug. She held on a minute before Evan pulled back, and Chief McArthur updated Evan on what little they knew.

"We're not even sure when Betty was last seen."

"I'll check the calendar at home again, see if I can find anything." Mary took a deep breath as she realized how much things had changed with Eleanor's phone call.

Evan stood and approached the chief, then started talking with him in muffled tones.

Surely all the mysteries Mary had solved while in Ivy Bay had prepared her for this very moment. Nothing was more important than finding Betty and getting her back safe and sound.

Mary stood and approached her nephew. "Evan, did she mention anything to you?"

"We haven't talked since Sunday."

Chief McArthur made a note. "Are you sure she didn't mention anything?"

"Yes, I'm sure. It was a normal after-church conversation. A quick catch-up on what the kids are doing. That kind of thing." Evan's baritone carried a strand of strain. "We have to find her. It's dark and cold out there. Who knows how whoever has Mom is treating her?"

"I promise we're working on it." Chief McArthur, with a compassionate look in his eyes, placed a hand on Evan's shoulder.

"If you're here," Evan said pointedly, "you aren't looking for her."

"That doesn't mean I don't have others searching. Right now, I need to collect information. Until the Boston PD arrives with the machines we need to track and record a ransom call, I'll remain here. Deputy Wadell will help me from the station and anywhere else I need him."

Mary had no doubt Chief McArthur would do all he could. But she would too.

Betty was her sister. Mary felt helpless yet convinced she had to do something. As she reviewed the words Eleanor had jotted down, she prayed something would come to her, but nothing did. It was just a string of words letting her know her sister was gone.

THREE

Chief McArthur's phone rang, and he stepped into the hallway to take the call. Evan approached Mary, tension curving his spine as he ran his fingers through his short brown hair. His normally proud bearing seemed beaten down by the events. Did she look the same?

Evan wrapped his arms around her, and she soaked in the comfort of knowing someone else was as concerned as she was. Then she noticed Eleanor and knew there were more than two people who cared about Betty. Eleanor couldn't sit still. She moved around the room, shifting items on already spotless surfaces, her face pale and expression taut.

Mary eased back from Evan and approached Eleanor. She touched the woman's arm, and Eleanor jerked. Only then did Mary notice the moisture in Eleanor's eyes. "She'll be okay, Eleanor."

"We don't know that." Eleanor swiped under her eyes.

"But we do. Less than an hour ago, you heard her. That means something."

Eleanor closed her eyes as if absorbing Mary's words and then sifting through them for truth. She nodded slowly, then opened her eyes and met Mary's concerned gaze. "You're right. I just feel helpless."

"We all do." Mary motioned Evan toward them. Betty needed them to work with the police and figure out what had happened. As she squeezed Eleanor's hand, she knew she had a formidable friend to help. "But when the kidnapper calls again, you'll be a crucial person."

Chief McArthur strode back into the room. "The Boston tech will be here in half an hour." He studied them a moment, then took a seat in the wing chair in front of the fireplace. "Why don't you all have a seat? I want to go through this one more time, just to make sure we've got everything."

Eleanor took the chair opposite him but fidgeted as she sat. "I don't know what more I can tell you. You've got the notes of what she told me."

"I appreciate that, Eleanor. I've learned through my career that the more we review a situation, the less likely we are to miss important details. At this time, anything you can tell me—even if you think you're repeating yourself—will be helpful."

Deputy Wadell leaned against the wall by the door, as if making sure no one left. Mary wondered at that. Eleanor wouldn't try to leave her own home, and she and Evan wanted to stay while there was any chance they could help locate Betty. A shiver shimmied through her at the thought of Betty out in the cold night. All alone and probably afraid. Mary prayed for Betty and then turned her thoughts back to the conversation around her.

Chief McArthur walked Eleanor through the call again. She rubbed her temples as she recalled the unusual timing of the call and the bland message.

"I would have thought she was calling with a question about our next book club meeting if it hadn't been for the words she used or the late hour. She didn't seem afraid or unsettled. Then that man came on." Eleanor shuddered. "That's when I knew it was serious and not some strange misunderstanding."

While Betty had a calm personality, Mary couldn't imagine the lack of emotion Eleanor described. Even with the mysteries Mary had solved and the puzzling circumstances she'd gotten herself in and out of, she imagined her response would be emotional. "Do you think he's drugged her, Chief?"

He used his pen to scratch his temple. "It's certainly possible. Or maybe Betty simply wanted to keep the situation from escalating. She's levelheaded, and I'd imagine she'd stay that way even in a situation like this."

Deputy Wadell nodded from his post. "She'd know getting hysterical wouldn't help anything and might make the situation worse."

"And you're sure you've remembered everything Betty said?" the chief asked Eleanor.

"As sure as I can be. I jotted down most of it as soon as I'd called you and Mary. I didn't want to forget anything that would be helpful. I've told you about the rest. Her 'hang ten' comment and the kidnapper's words." Her chin quivered, and she used a hand to cover it.

Mary wished Eleanor were on the couch next to her so she could slide an arm around her.

"Mom will be okay, won't she, Aunt Mary? Aunt Eleanor?" Evan's voice sounded strained.

Mary nodded but couldn't force words past the sudden lump in her throat.

Eleanor stared at the chief. "You *will* find her."

"I will do everything in my power, ma'am. You know that."

Eleanor appraised him and then nodded. "See that you do."

Evan pushed to his feet and started pacing the room. "Is there anything I can do? I hate waiting, but should I stay here, or is there something I can do to help?"

Chief McArthur studied him as if evaluating how to phrase something. "Do you have the ability to liquidate any assets if needed for a ransom?"

Evan blanched as he shook his head. "No. I've got a few investment accounts, but they are primarily college savings plans for the girls and a couple of retirement plans. I could get into the retirement accounts, but it wouldn't be quick."

"Mary?"

"Most of what I have is tied up in the bookshop. I might be able to get a line of credit." There had to be some banker in town who would recognize the value of what she had built with her business. Still, that would take time. Time Betty might not have.

Eleanor cleared her throat. "I have the money. That's why he called me, after all."

Mary knew she was right. The kidnapper knew Betty well enough to know she had a wealthy sister-in-law.

Chief McArthur made another note in his book, then looked up. "Evan, Mary, you should go home and get some sleep. If anything happens, I'll let you know immediately. Until we hear from the kidnapper, there isn't much we can do but wait. It's best if you try to get some sleep and be ready to go when we need you."

Mary hesitated. She didn't want to miss anything. Yet she knew if she didn't try to sleep, she wouldn't be much help in the morning. Part of her doubted she could get a wink of sleep no matter how much she needed it.

Chief McArthur looked at her knowingly. "I promise I'll call."

She nodded. He would. He was a trustworthy man. It just didn't help to know there was little she could do. However, if she headed home, she could check Betty's calendar again and think about anything Betty might have said that would tell Mary where her sister had headed that day. Maybe she could check on "hang ten" too.

Deputy Wadell's phone rang, and he stepped away. Mary gathered her things, and after hugging Eleanor and Evan, she stepped into the hallway to collect her coat.

As she opened the closet door, she overheard Deputy Wadell's low voice from the next room.

"Look, you know I'm working on it. There's not much I can do in the middle of the night when the bank is closed. What more do you expect?" There was a silence. "I'm working on a plan."

She took her coat off the hanger and turned toward the front door when the deputy stepped into the hallway. She nodded, hoping he wouldn't think she'd eavesdropped, but the way he stopped short indicated he knew she'd heard him.

A smile creased his face. "Hey, Mary, get some rest, okay? You'll be glad you did later." The smile remained firm on his face.

"I'll try." She offered a wobbly smile. "Thank you."

She did need to get home, to the place where she was more likely to find something that could help or see something that might trigger a thought. And maybe in the remembering, she'd think of something that led to Betty.

FOUR

W hen Mary walked through the door of her home, it
felt terribly empty.

"Betty?" Even though Mary knew there wouldn't be an
answer, she couldn't help herself. "Betty, are you home?"

Mary searched the first floor, then climbed the stairs to
her bedroom. Betty wasn't anywhere. Gus glanced up at her
from his post on her bed, his look suggesting he wasn't sure
why she would be searching the house. Then he laid his head
back down.

A chill settled over Mary, more than the cold of a March
night. It was the realization Betty really was not coming home.
Not until the kidnapper had whatever elusive amount he
wanted. Would Eleanor have enough money to satisfy him?

God, please keep Betty safe.

The one-sentence prayer became a mantra in her
mind, cycling over and over as she headed back downstairs.
Somewhere there was a clue that would help her find Betty.
Something that would lead the police to her sister.

The phone rang, and Mary hurried the rest of the way
downstairs and into the kitchen to answer it. *Could this be
Betty?*

"Hello?" She felt breathless, on edge, wondering what would happen.

"Mary, I hope it's not too late to call." Henry's voice was rich and soothing. Usually it would make her relax, but now all she wanted to do was weep. "Mary?"

"Hi, Henry." She drew in a shuddering breath. "I just got home."

"Did the police know anything?"

"Nothing helpful." She rubbed at the tension tightening her neck. "It's all so bizarre. How could this happen to Betty?"

"Do they have any idea where she is?"

"No, and I'm worried. She said an odd thing in her call to Eleanor. Something that simply doesn't make sense. And then the kidnapper came on the call."

She carried the phone to the kitchen table and sat in a chair. Somehow with Henry on the phone, the burden didn't seem quite so heavy.

"Can you fill me in?"

"I think so." Mary took a moment to clear her thoughts. "Betty called Eleanor about nine thirty tonight with a short message that she'd been kidnapped but was okay. She ended with the words *hang ten*. And then the kidnapper got on the phone and told Eleanor to start working with her bank. He'll call tomorrow with a ransom demand."

"Oh my."

Mary stood and walked to the sink. It was empty, and the breakfast dishes were loaded in the dishwasher, but she didn't notice any extra dishes that would indicate Betty had lunch at the house. "She must have left this morning."

"What?" Henry sounded confused.

"Sorry. I just noticed it doesn't look like Betty ate lunch here." Mary huffed out a breath. "The problem is I don't have any idea what she planned to do today. Maybe if I knew where she went and what she did, I could figure out when the kidnapper took her. Maybe that could lead us to him."

"If there's anything to find, you will."

"I hope so," she whispered quietly, but Henry must have heard.

"Would it help if I came over for a while? Kept you company?"

Mary had to smile at his thoughtfulness. "It's too late for that, Henry. Thank you, though."

"All I have tomorrow is an early morning fishing run. How about I come by first thing after that and help out?"

It would be nice to have company, someone to help with the hunt. "Thanks, Henry. It's so hard to believe she's not here."

Henry sighed. "We'll find her."

Mary nodded as his words wrapped around her.

"I promise, Mary."

"Thank you."

"Talk to you in the morning."

Mary held the phone an extra minute after Henry hung up. The house didn't feel quite as empty after his call. Yes, Betty was still missing, but Mary could start tracking her down. Tracing where Betty had gone today would be a good start. Chief McArthur would probably take the same steps, but Mary couldn't sit around waiting to hear what he learned.

The calendar mocked her from its spot on the wall. No matter how Mary looked at it, she couldn't find any note, jot, or doodle that gave any idea what Betty had done today.

After returning to her room, Mary sat on her bed and wrote out Betty's words from the call on a piece of notebook paper.

Hello, Eleanor,

I'm okay, but someone has kidnapped me and he wants to talk to you. Tell Mary that for now I'm okay. . . . Hang ten.

She studied the words, but they still made no sense to her. A tear trickled down her cheek, and she brushed it off. "God, please keep her safe."

Next she added the gist of the kidnapper's words. Eleanor was to start working with her bank and prepare for a ransom demand tomorrow morning. That told them nothing about the kidnapper or the amount he would ultimately request.

Mary stared at her notes but could think of nothing to add. She stood and began getting ready for bed for the second time that evening.

As she crawled under the covers, she kept a continuous prayer rising on Betty's behalf. She might not know where Betty was, but God did. And He would be there with her, in the midst of everything.

Hang ten. Hang ten. Hang ten.

As Mary lay in bed trying to fall asleep, the words kept cycling through her head. Over and over, like a never-ending mantra. *Hang ten.*

What was the significance of those words?

Mary sat up and grabbed her laptop. She yawned as she opened a search engine and entered "hang ten." Out of the top entries, most were for apparel or restaurants. But the *Urban*

Dictionary reinforced her original thought that the term was tied to surfing. Hanging the ten toes over the edge of the surfboard.

She puzzled over that. Why on earth would Betty have used that phrase? Her sister had never surfed a day in her life, at least not that Mary remembered. Yet for some reason, Mary sensed the phrase could be a key to finding her sister. What was Betty trying to communicate?

As her thoughts spun through the words, Mary couldn't figure out what to make of the phrase. The sinking feeling she was letting Betty down fell heavy upon her. Mary could only assume that—unless the kidnapper had dictated the phrase to Betty, which could be possible—it was something Betty would expect Mary to interpret.

As Mary drifted into a restless sleep, she couldn't decipher a thought, let alone the reason for the phrase.

Where was Betty?

Mary woke tossing and turning, the question burned into her thoughts. She sat up, glanced at the clock, and groaned when she read 2:19 AM. She shook her head, trying to clear the cobwebs of sleep and the fear that seemed to coat her. Betty wasn't here. A nameless kidnapper had taken her.

Kidnapper.

Someone who wanted money and had done his research. He'd known who to involve, a person with money and liquid assets.

Mary couldn't get the word out of her head. A *kidnapper* had taken her sister. But taken her from where? Another chill went through her spine as she considered whether the kidnapping had happened at the house. Was it possible?

Mary hadn't noticed any disturbance downstairs, but now as her brain churned, another thought hit her.

Where was Betty's car?

Mary groaned when she realized that, in her earlier search, she hadn't checked the garage. Since she always parked in the driveway, she hadn't entered the garage before turning in for the night.

She slipped on her robe, grabbed a large flashlight from the drawer of her bedside table, and put on slippers. Then she hurried down the stairs to the single-car garage. She didn't know whether to hope the car was there or not.

When she opened the door, the garage stood empty, with only a few leaves brushed into a corner.

Mary slowly closed the door and returned to the house. She felt wide awake, even though it was the middle of the night. She filled the teakettle and then turned on the burner. Maybe a cup of hot tea would calm her.

While she waited for the water to boil, she pulled a piece of paper out of the junk drawer. She wrote, "Where was Betty's car?"

It might not be in the garage, but it was somewhere. In the morning, she could focus on locating the car and tracing Betty's steps through the day. Somewhere she'd find a clue that would lead to Betty.

She doodled on the page as she tried to think where Betty could have gone. Betty often had meetings at the church, but nothing was listed on the calendar. Mary would start there and check with Betty's friends to see who had seen or talked to her.

Mary jotted a few notes, then poured water into her mug. She carried the steaming cup to bed and then tried to settle down to return to sleep. She must have dozed because the next time she looked around, the room was filled with the purple haze of morning.

The half-empty mug sat on her nightstand, the list tucked next to it. A shudder ran through her at the thought that Betty wasn't resting in her bedroom downstairs. Mary got ready as fast as she could, then headed downstairs where she made and filled a large thermos with coffee. She'd need the caffeine to get going after a night that had passed in fits and starts. She sat at the kitchen table long enough to finish a bowl of instant oatmeal while reading a psalm. The words comforted her, reminding her God could deliver Betty, a reminder she needed.

After placing her dishes in the dishwasher, she called Chief McArthur. He answered on the first ring.

"Chief McArthur here."

"Chief, this is Mary." He sounded as though he hadn't slept at all. "Any news?"

He sighed, and Mary's hopes fell. "Nothing. Not a word, but the tech has everything set up at Eleanor's, so we're ready to grab every word and track the call if the kidnapper follows through."

"I'm glad. This morning I'm going to retrace Betty's steps and see if I can find her car. It's not in the garage, which makes me pretty sure she wasn't taken from here."

"Good to know, but I already have officers keeping an eye out for her car. Mary, let us take care of this. We'll find her car if it's anywhere near Ivy Bay."

Mary worried her lower lip between her teeth. She didn't want to get in his way, but she needed to do something too. She couldn't wait passively by the phone while Betty was at the mercy of some kidnapper. "I promise I won't get in the way."

"Mary..." There was a hint of resigned frustration tinting the chief's words. He knew her too well to be surprised she was determined to find Betty.

"Thanks, Chief." Mary hung up, then grabbed a banana to take along. If she could somehow retrace Betty's steps, she might find the location of her car and where she was last seen. While the police might find the same information, surely it was better if they all worked to find Betty. The first forty-eight hours were critical in finding kidnapping victims, Mary had heard, and the hours were speeding past. Right now, nobody knew enough to find Betty without a lot of hard work and shoe leather.

Mary shrugged into her coat, hiked her purse over her shoulder, and grabbed her keys. Gus strode up the hall toward her.

"I'm sorry, Gus, but you have to stay home. I have no idea where I'll go, so it's best that you stay here."

He sniffed and turned his back on her. Some days that cat acted as if he understood every word she said.

Shaking her head at his attitude, Mary opened the front door expecting to see the sun rising. Since it was only seven forty-five, the school bus wouldn't have made its circuit yet. When she stepped onto the porch, she froze. Dorothy Johnson and Amy Stebble sat on two folding chairs on the lawn, hands joined as they prayed.

"Lord, keep her safe. Amen." Dorothy looked up, brows down as she studied Mary. "Are you okay, friend?"

Mary nodded, then shook her head. "What are you doing here?"

"Tricia Miles called first thing this morning with the news about Betty. She couldn't come since she had an appointment, but Amy and I wanted to pray here...for you and Betty. Just like you've prayed for us so many times."

Amy nodded. "There are many moments in my life that your prayers helped carry me through. The least I could do was come and provide the same support to you." Amy glowed with certainty as she pushed to her feet. "Can we pray with you before I head to the elementary school?"

Dorothy was dressed well, her stylish hair perfect and her ever-present pearls in place. "Please join us, Mary."

As Mary stepped nearer, her two friends circled her in a hug. Amy led. "Father, we thank You for Mary and Betty, and for the special bond they share. We ask that You would keep Betty safe and that You would fill both of these ladies with peace. Let them see Your hand of protection and guidance in their lives. Be very present.

"Lord, I also ask that You would comfort Mary. It's hard to not know what is happening with a loved one. But You know. Give Mary that assurance. Give her wisdom and insight and lead the police to Betty."

"Amen." It was the only word Mary could push past the boulder squeezed in her throat. "Thank you."

Amy gave her an extra squeeze, then grabbed her folding chair and walked to the car.

A moment later, Dorothy stepped back. "If you need anything, call. You're not alone, Mary. Now go do what you do best. Go solve this riddle and find Betty."

As she watched her friends leave, Mary realized the truth of Dorothy's statement. No matter what she felt, she wasn't alone.

FIVE

Mary slipped into her car, still touched by the amazing generosity of her friends. To think they made time in their busy mornings not just to pray but to come and let her know they prayed. She had forgotten how encouraging it could be to simply know you weren't alone.

She hummed along to a praise chorus on the radio that reminded her that God was sovereign. She needed that message during the short drive to the bookstore. Normally, the thought of going to her store brought joy. This morning, she couldn't shove back her concern for Betty. As her breath spiraled in front of her in the cold, she wondered if the kidnapper had provided Betty with a warm place to sleep. Would he give her something to eat for breakfast? Fortunately, Betty didn't need certain medicine at specified times, but that was small comfort.

She longed to dial Betty's cell and have her sister's upbeat voice on the other end of the call. The police would do all they could to find her, but Mary couldn't help if she stayed in her car. First, she needed to drop off the list she'd made for Rebecca Mason the night before. Rebecca was her right hand at the shop and could handle anything that came up while

Mary was out. Still, she wanted to leave her a note with a few instructions and a brief explanation of why she'd be gone.

Mary had also brought a few things to leave at the store so she could use it as a base of operations without returning home. Mary parked and climbed from her car, dragging a couple of bags after her. As she stepped onto the sidewalk, Susan Crosby hurried out of Sweet Susan's Bakery next door.

"Mary." Susan's dark hair was flecked with flour as though emphasizing the hours she'd already logged getting items ready for the bakery shelves. "I'm so upset about Betty. How are you holding up?"

"How did you find out?" Mary couldn't imagine how the word had spread so quickly.

"Pastor Miles was in for a muffin before heading to the church. He mentioned the trouble with Betty." One of Susan's hands worried the edges of her apron. "I can't imagine how you're holding up."

"As well as I can." She was barely holding it together, but she put on a smile for her friend.

Susan released her apron and slipped a small pastry box topped with a bag toward her. "I've been watching for you all morning. I know this isn't much, but the bag has a cranberry-orange muffin. I can't imagine you've thought about food today. I also put a lemon chiffon cupcake in the box for when you need fuel later." Mary accepted the items and found herself engulfed in a big hug.

"Thank you." Her words were muffled by Susan's shoulder.

"It's such a small thing. Know I am praying for you and Betty. She's such a dear." Susan put her hands near her face and waved them. "The whole idea that she could be kidnapped is ridiculous, but one look at you tells me it's true. What is the world coming to?"

What indeed?

"What else can I do for you?"

Mary considered Susan's question carefully. "Could you ask your customers when they last saw Betty? We need to re-create what she did yesterday, so we can figure out where and when she was taken."

"Of course I'll do that." Susan gave her another hug, this one shorter than the first, then followed a customer into her shop.

Mary unlocked the front door to her bookstore. The building was more than two hundred years old, and she liked the way it creaked and groaned. Sunbeams already filtered through the bay window by the door, hinting at the retreat the store was for those who loved good books.

She settled the pastry box and bag on the marble counter, then pulled from her handbag the list she'd created during the night. As she reviewed the list, she realized there was nothing on it Rebecca couldn't figure out on her own, but it made Mary feel better to leave it anyway.

After leaving the list where Rebecca would be sure to see it, along with a quick note explaining her absence, Mary retrieved her treats from Susan and walked out the door. After she tucked them in her car, she turned toward the church.

As Mary walked toward Grace Church, she prayed Pastor Miles would be available this morning. It was reasonable to think Betty might have stopped by the church at some point the prior morning. If so, Pastor Miles might know where she'd headed next. It was a slim chance, but it was the best she had.

Mary approached the church. In typical New England style, it was painted white up to its tall spire, which could be seen for miles. Most mornings, Mary thought the church and setting were striking. Others agreed, because during the height of the tourist season, the sidewalk across from the church was often lined with people taking pictures of the building. This morning, she was simply grateful to see Pastor Miles's car parked next to the steps.

Mary headed for the office entrance. As soon as she entered the reception area, she heard the pastor's voice from inside his office, the words signaling the end to a phone call. She walked to the room and rapped lightly on the open door.

"Mary, hi. Come on in." As she entered the office, Pastor Miles stood and walked around his desk. He put an arm around her shoulders and eased her to a chair. "I've been praying without ceasing since you called."

"Thank you, Pastor."

"How can I help?"

The office door leading to the reception area opened, and Mary turned to see Margie, the church secretary, slip inside with an exaggerated shudder. "Boy, am I ready for March to leave like a lamb." She shook out her coat and hung it in a closet, but startled when she turned. She hurried into the office. "Mary, how are you?"

Mary shrugged. "As well as I can be."

"Oh?" Margie leaned against the doorframe and gave Mary her full attention.

"I haven't told her anything." Pastor Miles shrugged. "I thought I'd fill her in when she arrived."

"Tell me what?"

"Betty called Eleanor last night. She's been kidnapped," Mary said. The words seemed so bald, yet how else could she tell people? Cushioning the truth didn't change the reality of what had happened.

"Good gracious!" Margie covered her mouth and stared at Mary.

"She was about to tell me what I can do to help." Pastor Miles motioned to the chairs in front of his desk. "Why don't we have a seat?"

Margie nodded and sat in a chair next to Mary. Her hand still covered her mouth as she shook her head. "Are you sure? I can't remember us ever having a kidnapping in Ivy Bay."

"Unfortunately, I am sure." Mary sighed and shrugged her shoulders, a feeble attempt to release the tension that gripped her. "Did either of you see Betty yesterday? I'm trying to retrace her steps and am pretty much at a loss about where to start."

Pastor Miles thought a minute, then shook his head. "I don't remember seeing her."

"Don't you, Pastor?" Margie pointed to a stack of baskets barely visible behind her desk. "Betty came in yesterday to drop off some clothes for the women's shelter clothing drive."

"Oh, that's right. She didn't stay long."

Mary sighed. Someone had seen Betty, and she'd been fine. She leaned toward the secretary. "What did she say?"

"Nothing much. Just that she was donating some items."

"Not some." Pastor Miles pointed toward the stack that appeared to lean somewhat precariously. "She must have brought in five laundry baskets of clothes. It will be a huge blessing to the clothing closet."

"Do you remember when she arrived?"

Margie got up and looked at her desk calendar, then returned to her seat. "I'd say between ten thirty and eleven. She was here before the men came to set up for their lunch prayer time."

Mary had left the house about nine fifteen, and Betty had still been in her robe and pajamas. Ten thirty seemed a reasonable time for her to get ready and make her way to the church.

Margie sank lower in her seat. "I wish I could be more help."

"You've already told me more than I knew before. Thank you. By chance, did Betty say where she was headed next?"

"I'm not sure I remember." Margie crossed her arms and frowned. "Wait...I remember now. She was headed to the Black & White Diner for lunch. I remember it made me hungry for a stack of their pancakes. She mentioned meeting someone for lunch."

"Did she say who?" Mary held her breath, hoping Margie would say yes.

"No, I'm afraid she didn't, and I didn't ask."

At least Mary knew where Betty had gone next and that she apparently had plans to meet someone. "Did she mention anything for after lunch?"

Margie shook her head. "Sorry, no she didn't." Margie's skin paled as she squeezed Mary's hand. "I can't imagine what you're going through. And poor Betty."

"You've already helped a great deal." Mary swallowed and tried to push back her fear for Betty with a prayer for protection. She was glad she could trust that God knew exactly where her sister was and cared for her even now. "I don't know if I'll ever understand how this happened."

"What can we do, Mary?" Pastor Miles watched her closely.

"Prayer is the best thing. Ladies from my prayer group were waiting on my front lawn this morning."

"That's wonderful."

"It was. Until I know more about where she was taken and where we should look, I don't know what else to suggest. Except to ask anyone who calls or comes in about the last time they saw Betty. We can use that information to track where she went."

Margie jotted a note on her calendar. "I'll be sure to do that. I know everyone will want to help."

"If I learn there's anything else that could help, I'll let you know." Mary stood and gathered her purse and coat.

"Please do, Mary." Pastor Miles stood and stepped around his desk. "The phone has been ringing since I arrived this morning. Seems the Ivy Bay grapevine is in action. I wanted to talk to you before calling people back so I knew best how we could help." Pastor Miles gave her a one-armed hug. "We're here for you in any way you need. Your church family loves you and Betty. And God's got her in His hands."

"I know." Mary leaned further into the pastor's embrace before pulling away. She really did understand at the core of her being that God held Betty. Relaxing into that knowledge was much harder.

SIX

—◆◆◆—

Mary had stepped out of Pastor Miles's office and was walking toward the main entrance when she saw Deputy Wadell heading toward her. His uniform was rumpled, as if he hadn't found time to change into a fresh one. The dark circles under his eyes emphasized that he'd probably stayed up most of the night.

Betty's kidnapping was affecting many in town, almost a ripple effect as the word spread. As Mary met Deputy Wadell's gaze, she wondered if his unkempt appearance had anything to do with what he'd been talking about on the phone last night. Betty's kidnapping could only add weight to whatever else was happening in his personal life.

"Good morning, Deputy. Are you holding up okay?"

"I'm more concerned about you." He glanced toward the window. "I noticed your car outside. Thought I'd stop and see if you need anything." Concern shaded his eyes.

"That's very kind. I'm just trying to trace Betty."

"Have you learned anything?

"Margie told me Betty visited the church at around ten thirty or eleven yesterday morning and planned to visit the Black & White Diner from here."

"Good to know. Anything else?"

Mary didn't want to tell him that was it. The way he'd asked for more made her discovery seem small and empty. Yet she knew it was more than she'd known.

Margie returned to her desk, and her smile widened when she saw Deputy Wadell. "I thought I heard another voice. How are you this morning? Need a cup of coffee?"

"Not now, though it's kind of you to offer."

"I'll keep a fresh pot going today. Stop any time you need more." Margie got a twinkle in her eyes, one Mary knew from experience meant she'd had an idea that would require a lot of work. "I'd like to help organize a search, Deputy. People will call here to find out what they can do. We're the perfect headquarters for organizing people to look for Betty."

Deputy Wadell seemed to consider the idea but then shook his head. "I don't think so."

"Why not?"

The deputy took off his cap, rubbed a hand over his crew cut, and then set the cap back in place. "We don't have enough information. We don't even know where she disappeared from, which means we don't have a place to start the search. At this point, it would be a waste of effort, effort we should save for when we know more."

Margie jutted out her chin and crossed her arms. "We could cover a lot of ground."

"And waste a lot of time." He shook his head. "An organized search is a feat of manpower. Someone has to plot where to search, who does what, track results, and more. You don't just snap your fingers and start looking. That can be worse than no search at all. We don't want to have to repeat a search after people have already volunteered. When we know more, it might make sense. Right now, it would be a waste of time and man power. Trust me."

Mary suspected he was right, but the idea of doing nothing still bothered her. "What about the importance of finding a kidnapping victim in the first forty-eight hours?"

"Sure, that's important, but we have to know where to look." Deputy Wadell rubbed his chin and sighed. "You have to understand—there's crucial information we don't have. Nobody saw her taken. Let us do our job without getting distracted by a premature search."

"All right. I'll start by heading to the diner. Margie, maybe you can build a list of those ready to help search. Then if the time comes, we'll know who to call."

"Got it." Margie made a notation on her notepad. "It's the least we can do."

Deputy Wadell's phone belted out a jazz tune, and he pulled it from his pocket. After a glance at the screen, he turned to Mary. "Mrs. Fisher." Then he answered the phone and walked to the narthex.

After again thanking Margie for her help, Mary decided she'd take a minute to pray in the chapel before walking to the diner. If she ran into Deputy Wadell again before he left, she could ask him if he'd had time to research "hang ten" as he'd intended. Maybe his results were more interesting than hers.

As she made her way to the chapel, the tense sound of Deputy Wadell's voice reached her from a room off the hall, a tone so unlike what she usually heard him use. She glanced into the narthex as she passed on her way to the chapel. His back was turned as he faced the window, one hand plugging an ear while the other held his cell. Mary paused, careful not to disturb him. Could the call have something to do with Betty?

Air hissed from his mouth. "I told you I'll get everything taken care of. Don't worry about the loan. I'll find a way." He was trying to keep his voice quiet, but the tension in it betrayed his efforts. His voice rose a little more. "You know I just need more time. Work's crazy right now."

Mary began to second-guess waiting as Deputy Wadell's voice continued to rise. If the call involved Betty, surely Deputy Wadell would have headed back to where he'd left Mary. Plus, he was clearly upset, and she didn't want to embarrass him. She slipped away before he saw her.

A moment later, Mary entered the chapel. The room was smaller than the sanctuary but large enough to have a nook of comfy stuffed chairs and, in another area, a circle of folding chairs. Soft, multicolored light streamed through a stained-glass window. Entering the space, her spirit quieted as it did so often during her weekly prayer group meeting. She sat in one of the stuffed chairs and took a few minutes to meditate on the Lord's promise that He kept His children engraved on His hand. She loved that image of Betty being squarely in the middle of His palm. Her breath slowed with each passing moment.

When she slipped from the chapel, Deputy Wadell's cruiser still sat in the parking lot, next to her sedan. She glanced toward the office and noticed him pacing in front of the narthex windows.

As she turned back to her car, she wondered where Betty's was. If Mary's search at the Black & White Diner didn't lead to further clues, she could drive Ivy Bay's roads, looking for Betty's car. What else could she do?

Mary hurried across Meeting House Road and past Meeting House Grocers. As Mary passed, proprietor Kaley Court hurried out, her brown hair slipping from its ponytail.

"Mary, I am so glad to see you." Kaley's words tumbled out even quicker than her normal eager pace. "Please tell me the rumor isn't true."

"I'm afraid it is."

"How are you holding up?"

"As well as I can."

Kaley clucked her tongue. "I have some fresh coffee at the deli. Would a cup help? I imagine you didn't sleep a wink."

"Very sweet of you, Kaley. I've already had a thermos full, but thank you. Any more and my worries would only compound."

"Oh, you poor thing! And poor Betty!" Kaley wrapped her thin arms around Mary in a hug.

Mary returned the hug and then took a step back. "I am worried about her. I just need to keep looking for her."

"Of course you do." Kaley nodded, her brown eyes intent. "Say, you know Pipp? Our golden retriever?"

Mary nodded as she pictured the gorgeous but somewhat unruly dog.

"Well, I was thinking. I want to help. Maybe I could take Pipp out to look. You see it on the news all the time, how dogs can be a great help in finding missing people. I'm sure Pipp could do that."

Mary's breath caught in her chest at the idea that a search dog might be needed and useful. As she thought about the stories she'd read and news she'd seen, it seemed that most of the time, dogs were brought in to find bodies. That idea truly frightened her and was far beyond where Mary was willing to allow her thoughts to go. Instead, she fought to hold on to the peace she'd gained in the chapel. Betty had been fine last night when she called. Eleanor had been crystal clear with her opinion that Betty hadn't been harmed. Surely that hadn't changed in the twelve hours since that call.

"Are you all right, Mary?" Concern clouded Kaley's eyes as she leaned toward Mary. "I didn't mean to upset you."

"I'll be fine, Kaley." She had to keep working through Betty's day yesterday. "But I'm not sure I'm ready for that kind of search yet. In fact, Deputy Wadell said it's too early since we don't know where the kidnapper grabbed Betty. I've seen those news stories too, but it seems they're always looking for people who are—" She couldn't bring herself to say the word.

Luckily, Kaley raised her hand to suggest she understood. "Don't say another word. I didn't think of it that way, because I thought he could just pick up the scent of her clothes— who knows, maybe the kidnapper has her somewhere nearby and Pipp could find her by the smell of her shampoo or something. If you or the police decide to search and Pipp can be helpful, please let me know."

"Thank you. Did you see Betty yesterday?"

"I did, actually. But only for a minute. She came in for a bottle of water. I didn't get a chance to talk to her. If I'd known what would happen . . . but yesterday felt like every other day."

"Do you remember what time that was?"

Kaley thought for a moment, her brows crinkling as she did. "Sometime in the morning. Before ten o'clock, because that's when our delivery arrived. It kind of separates my days."

"Did she say anything?"

"Not out of the ordinary. It was a typical grocery-store conversation. Paper or plastic? That kind of thing." Kaley straightened her apron as she glanced down the street. "But I do remember seeing her again, half an hour or so later, when she walked back by the store."

"Do you know which direction she was headed? Was anyone with her?"

Kaley pointed in the direction of the diner. "I don't think anyone was with her, but I can't be entirely sure. The delivery truck had arrived by then, and I had to check the order as the boxes came in. All those boxes and containers."

Mary could imagine the chaos that would erupt with an order the size that Kaley received at the grocery store. Just getting a few boxes of books a couple of times during the month could throw off her day in the most delightful way. "Thanks, Kaley."

Mary was about to bid good-bye to Kaley when the grocery's door opened and a man backed out, two cloth shopping bags bulging with items and hanging from his hands. Before she could get out of his way, he collided with Mary, and the breath whooshed from her as she stumbled against the building. Kaley steadied her as the man staggered to a stop. He was average height but still taller than Mary's petite frame. There was nothing that stood out about him, yet he seemed vaguely familiar, like someone she'd seen before but never been introduced to or really noticed.

He turned to her, his dark eyes carrying a distant look as if he were in the middle of deep thoughts that had distracted him. He dipped his chin in her direction. "My apologies."

Before she could reply, he stepped away and hurried toward a red sedan.

Kaley watched the man walk away, before turning to Mary. "Are you all right?"

"I'm fine." Mary straightened, then turned to Kaley. "Well, I'd better get to the diner."

"Remember. Pipp is available to help if you need him." Kaley turned to go back into her store.

Mary began the short walk to the diner. Could Pipp help? If Betty hadn't been found or returned by early evening, Mary might well be willing to try something as crazy as a search led by a dog.

She pulled out her phone and called Chief McArthur. He answered almost immediately.

"Mary?" The chief sounded intense, focused, and busy.

"Hi, Chief. I'm still retracing Betty's steps yesterday." She filled him in on what she had learned from Margie and Kaley. Then she said, "Did Deputy Wadell mention whether he'd looked into 'hang ten'?"

"No. We're running as hard as we can, but there's nothing new here." Chief McArthur paused as voices spoke up in the background. A moment later, he was back. "Sorry about that. The kidnapper hasn't called, so we're in a waiting game. We don't have much to work with yet."

The chief hung up to take another call, and Mary stopped in front of the diner. Its awning cast a pool of shade across the brick front and the red newspaper box that sat next to the door.

She stooped down to purchase a paper. A small box inserted into the top right-hand corner of the front page requested help finding a missing Ivy Bay woman. Mary hadn't had the time to read the newspaper that morning, and seeing that small box with Betty's name in large letters stopped her in her tracks. If Johanna Montgomery had managed to get that snippet squeezed in on such short notice, then people across Ivy Bay and the surrounding area knew about the kidnapping and would watch for Betty—if they knew her. Johanna had likely heard something was happening on the police scanner, and her small piece explained how the grapevine had worked so well.

Well, the more people who knew, the more people who could help find Betty. Someone knew something, and the farther the word spread, the more likely that person would know to come forward. Mary should call Johanna and see if they could run a photo, in case the police didn't find Betty soon.

Mary tucked the newspaper under her arm and entered the Black & White Diner. The aroma of rich coffee blended with sizzling bacon and a hint of chocolate from the diner's famous chocolate chip pancakes. Quite a few tables held patrons, half with breakfast and half with an early lunch set in front of them.

Nicole Hancock, hair swept up in a sleek ponytail, smiled as she hurried past Mary. "I'll be right with you. Grab any table you like."

Mary opted for a seat at the counter. That allowed Nicole to chat while pouring coffee and preparing drinks at the counter. Mary set the paper on the counter and rescanned the article. After collecting a couple of plates from the pass-through window, Nicole carried them to a table. She wiped another table clean on her way back and dropped her rag in a bucket of bleach water before grabbing the coffeepot and a mug.

As soon as she set the coffee mug down, Mary placed her hand on top of it. "Nicole, could I have a mug of tea? I've already had too much coffee this morning."

Compassion filled Nicole's turquoise eyes as she flipped her blonde ponytail over her shoulder. She set the pot back on the burner and then grabbed a container of tea bags. "I bet it has been one of those mornings." She set the tea bags in front of Mary, then grabbed a carafe of hot water and filled the mug. "I really don't even know what to say."

Mary selected a tea bag and dropped it in the hot water. "Were you working when Betty came here yesterday?"

"Sure. You know I rarely escape this place."

"Watch it, young lady." Her father's voice came from the kitchen where the clank of dishes continued.

Nicole made a face and then shrugged. "You know how fathers are. Always eavesdropping on their children." She said the last sentence more loudly over her shoulder. Then her expression sobered. "Betty seemed her normal self yesterday. She was as sweet as always, smiling and unconcerned once the young man she was meeting arrived."

"Order up."

"I'll be right back."

Young man? Mary swirled the tea bag through the water and then sipped her tea, letting it brace her as she waited for Nicole to return. What young man? Who could Betty have met? She hadn't mentioned any such plans, and there weren't many young men Mary could imagine her sister meeting for an early lunch. Mary's phone rang, and she scrambled through her purse until she found it. "Hello?"

"Aunt Mary."

"Evan! Have you heard anything?" Mary clutched the phone to her ear and plugged her other so she could hear her nephew over the clanking silverware and plates.

"I was hoping you had." Evan sounded more tired than Mary had ever heard him, his usual upbeat tone missing. "I don't know anything new since last night."

Mary clucked an acknowledgment. "I think we're all in that position. Nothing to report other than Betty stopped at the church and diner yesterday." It took only a moment to fill him in on what she'd learned.

"Where is she, Aunt Mary?" His distress deepened his voice. "It's been more than twelve hours since Mom and the kidnapper called. I'm worried about her."

"I know, Evan. I am too."

"I've driven around, but it seems kind of useless."

Mary looked down at the menu she'd practically memorized. How could she offer hope to her nephew when she carried the same fears and concerns? "We'll find her. Looking for her car was a good idea. Did you see it?"

"No." She heard a shuddering sigh and could picture him squaring his shoulders as she'd seen so many times when Evan confronted a challenge or unpleasant task. "I still can't imagine who would do this."

"I can't either." When she couldn't sleep, she'd lain in bed for what felt like half the night trying to identify a suspect, but she'd drawn a blank. "We have to trust we'll find her."

"You're right. We have to. The police are good at what they do, and you're looking too."

His words settled over her. "Yes, I am. And God is with her."

"I know you're right. Just... You'll let me know if you learn anything?"

"Of course. You do the same. Did your mom mention who she met for lunch yesterday?"

"Lunch?" Evan paused. "No, she didn't mention any plans to me."

"Me neither." She startled as a hand settled on her shoulder. She turned to look at who it could be and smiled. "I'll call you back soon, Evan." She hung up as Henry eased onto the vacant stool next to her. "Fancy seeing you here."

"I saw a certain vehicle parked across the street. You weren't at the store, so I took my chances." He studied her as he crossed his arms and leaned on the counter. "You were supposed to call."

"Actually, you were supposed to call me." She rubbed a point on her temple that throbbed. As she dug through her purse for some aspirin, she cleared a lump from her throat. "I'm trying to retrace Betty's steps yesterday."

"Learn anything?"

"She stopped at Meeting House Grocers, church, and then here. Sounds like she met someone for lunch, but I don't know who yet. Oh, and Kaley has volunteered Pipp for a search."

Henry rubbed her arm, a smooth, comforting motion. "It'll be okay."

"If one more person tells me that..." She bit down against the frustration.

"Isn't that what you told Evan?"

"Yes, but he needs to hear his mother will be found."

"So do you. She's your sister and best friend." Henry's words couldn't be truer. He leaned toward her, close enough for her to smell the salty sea he'd brought in with him. "You will find her. And I'm going to help." He waggled his eyebrows. "With a chauffeur like me, you can cover territory twice as fast."

A small wave of relief went through her. Henry's company was the best offer of help she'd received all day. "And give Deputy Wadell a reason to pull us over?"

"Aw, the last time he did that, I only got a warning. Today we have extenuating circumstances."

Nicole returned behind the counter. "Sorry about the delay, Mary. Hi, Henry. Need a cup of coffee?"

"Biggest you have."

Nicole grabbed a clean mug, set it in front of Henry, and filled it to the brim. "Would you like fresh water and a new tea bag?"

"Thanks, Nicole." After Nicole replaced her cold mug, Mary doctored the tea and took a sip. Nicole wiped the counter, and Mary set down her mug and focused on the young woman. "You mentioned there was a young man with Betty. Did you know him?"

Nicole thought a moment. "I don't think so."

"What did he look like?"

"He seemed pretty average. Nice. Probably college-aged, and I think he had a college sweatshirt on."

"Do you remember the college?"

Nicole stared out the window but shook her head. "I don't remember. Betty struck me as happy to see him, and they seemed comfortable with each other. Nothing awkward or uncertain about their interactions."

Who could it be?

"Wait a minute." Nicole looked at Mary. "She did mention the young man's name. I can't believe I forgot that. She said his name was D.J."

Of course. D.J. He was the only college-aged young man Mary knew. But why would he meet Betty for lunch and not invite Mary? It seemed the sort of meeting Betty would have mentioned to Mary. "Was it an MIT sweatshirt?"

"Yes, that's it!" Nicole thought another moment. "Even though it was early, we already had a good-size lunch crowd. I was running all over the diner taking orders and delivering plates. But Betty stopped me. You know how friendly she is. Said she wanted to introduce me to her cousin's son."

Mary was surprised Betty would have lunch with D.J. and not mention it—even in passing—to Mary. Did that mean they hadn't wanted Mary to join them? What possible reason could they have for keeping her from the conversation?

Mary knew one way to find out. As soon as she left, she'd call D.J. and drive over to Cambridge to see him, if that was what it took. "Did Betty talk to anyone else while she was here?"

"Sure. A few people stopped by her table to say hi, and Deputy Wadell talked with her for a few minutes." She shrugged. "I know that's not much help."

"It's more than I knew before." Mary would need to ask Deputy Wadell about their conversation. Why hadn't he mentioned seeing Betty at the diner? "Did Betty mention where she was headed next?"

"Not exactly. She said something about working on her next project." Nicole frowned, then shrugged. "I'm sorry, but that's all I remember." She wiped the already clean counter, and Mary waited, giving her time to remember something, anything more. "You know, one more person stopped by. I didn't recognize him, though I'm not sure he actually said anything to Betty. But he talked with D.J for a few minutes." The girl looked past Mary as if trying to re-create the scene. "I'm just not sure. As I said, there was an early lunch rush yesterday. Enough to keep me moving."

"I appreciate everything you remember. What did this person look like?"

"He was about as tall as Henry. He hit the same mark on the strip next to the door." Mary turned and looked at the height measure. "He was also wearing a college hoodie. I think it was MIT too."

"Everything helps, Nicole." So Betty ate with D.J., and during that meal, Deputy Wadell and another man, possibly connected to MIT, stopped by her table.

"Order up." The brusque call had Nicole looking over her shoulder, then back at Mary.

"I wish I could be more help."

"You've helped a lot, Nicole. Thanks." Mary patted Nicole's hand. Then the waitress moved back to the window to fetch the order. Mary turned to Henry. "So you're serious about chauffeuring me?"

"Absolutely." He pulled his keys from his jacket pocket. "Just tell me where to go."

Nicole returned and slid two Styrofoam cups, one with a telltale tea tag hanging from the side, across the counter. "Take these with you."

"Thank you." Mary collected her things and the to-go cup of tea, and turned around on the stool. She froze when she noticed the man who'd bumped into her at the grocery store sitting at a table behind her, his head turning away from her when they made eye contact as if he'd been watching and listening. He'd been getting in his car when she walked to the diner, yet now he was sitting there paying attention to her. Why? Had he listened to her conversations? As she tried to remember everything she'd said or heard in the last fifteen minutes, none of it should interest anyone who didn't know or care about Betty.

So who was he?

SEVEN

The man glanced down. He reached for his mug of coffee and slid a steno-size notebook to the side, almost out of view under a plate.

"Mary?" Henry's voice drew her attention from the man. "Where do you want to start?"

"I need to call my cousin. But first I need to talk to someone."

"Want me to take your tea to the car?"

"Sure. I should only be a minute."

Shifting her purse strap, Mary covered the few feet to the man's table as Henry paid and then headed to his car. She waited a moment, but the man who'd collided with her didn't look up or acknowledge her.

She cleared her throat. "Hello. I'm Mary Fisher."

The man finally glanced up at her. "Do I know you?"

"I don't know. I own the bookstore across the street." She didn't see a flicker of recognition, which struck her as strange. Downtown Ivy Bay was small enough that her shop was hard to miss. "You ran into me earlier outside the grocery store."

His eyes widened slightly, and he stumbled to his feet. "My apologies. I'm afraid I get lost in my thoughts occasionally and miss what's happening." He gestured toward her. "You aren't hurt, are you?"

"Oh. No." She shook her head. "I'm just fine. Are you from Ivy Bay?"

"Not really, no." He pulled his wallet from his back pocket and tugged a bill free. After he tossed it next to his plate, he grabbed his notebook and nodded to Mary. "If you'll excuse me, I need to make an appointment."

"Of course." Mary watched him hurry from the building, curiosity rooting her in place.

Nicole buzzed by. "Do you need anything else?"

"No, but thanks, Nicole."

She wove between the tables to the door. Henry waited beside his car, the engine purring.

"Everything all right?" He looked at her with the intense focus that made her feel he wanted to see into her.

"Yes. I'll call D.J. Then we'll know where to go next."

"Were you able to talk to the person you wanted?"

"It wasn't what I expected." Though if he probed, she wouldn't be able to explain. The gentleman couldn't be interested in her discussion with Nicole. If anything, he'd heard a reference to Betty and been curious. He'd been oblique about whether he was from Ivy Bay. Why not just say yes or no? If he was from the town, he could be concerned that a local resident had been kidnapped. Things like that didn't happen here. Not with the regularity that would cause one to be an ignorable event.

Besides, the Black & White Diner was a popular place for people to eat. It probably didn't mean a thing that he was there at the same time she was. Yet his evasiveness and the way he didn't offer his name after she gave hers roused her suspicions rather than calming them.

She felt a slight pressure at her elbow and turned toward Henry. She accepted the cup he held. "Let's head to the house. I'll call D.J. and think a minute about what Betty might have meant when she told Nicole about her 'next project.'"

He gestured toward his vintage blue-and-white 1953 Chevy Bel Air convertible. "Do you want to drive your car there, and I'll meet you at your house?"

That made good sense. "That would be great."

"I'll see you at your house, then."

"Thank you."

Mary crossed the street to her car, set her purse in the backseat, then settled in the front and put the cup of tea in a holder. She dug her phone out of her pocket and scrolled through her contacts for D.J. His name didn't show up. She must not have programmed him in her contacts. His mother, Jean, could give her his phone number, but when Mary dialed, the call went to voice mail. Mary sank against the seat and thought. Betty probably had D.J.'s number. Maybe she'd added it to the phone book at the house. Mary started the car and prayed she was right.

When she walked into her house, she couldn't shake the hope that somehow this was all a mistake and that Betty would be sitting at the kitchen table doing her devotions or eating a bowl of soup. Then they could laugh together about the mix-up. But as Mary opened the door, Gus was the only one to meet her. She left the door cracked because Henry was pulling up, then went to the kitchen, Gus shadowing her steps. It almost seemed he was worried something would happen to her.

The front door squeaked, and Henry's footsteps followed her down the hall.

"Mary?"

"Come on back to the kitchen." She opened a drawer and dug out a small address book Betty had maintained for as long as Mary could remember. After flipping through the pages, she found D.J.'s number. A moment later, she dialed the number and then waited for him to answer.

"Hello?" The tight voice didn't sound like Jean's son.

"Is D.J. in? This is his mother's cousin, Mary Fisher."

"Who?"

Mary explained again.

There was a muffled sound, then the voice came back. "I haven't seen him, but I've been in and out."

"Do you know when he'll be back? It's imperative I talk to him today."

"He doesn't have classes this week, so he's usually around. You should try later."

"Do you have another number? It's urgent that I reach him."

"Look, I don't like giving out friends' numbers without permission. I can let him know you called."

"Thanks." Mary gave the young man her number and hung up.

"You don't look too happy."

She startled and then looked at Henry. "D.J. wasn't home. I don't want to wait, but he lives about an hour away."

"I don't mind driving, unless you have something else to do here."

That was the problem. She had tracked Betty to the diner and knew she'd seen D.J. Beyond that, Mary was at a loss about what her sister had done next. She sank onto a stool. "I guess we could drive around here. See if we find her car."

"Or we can leave that to the police and drive over to this young man's apartment."

"I wish I could figure out what her project was."

"Might it have had anything to do with D.J.?"

"Maybe."

Mary tapped her chin and studied the calendar. Sometimes Betty doodled on it, but other than an abundance of flowers, there wasn't much on it. Yesterday had remained blank...no matter how many times Mary looked at it, nothing appeared. She idly studied the flower doodles around the calendar. A thought occurred. Betty might have been ready to plan her flower beds.

That idea had potential. Betty took great pride, and rightly so, in her beautiful beds. She was always experimenting with new flowers and trying fresh arrangements of plants and colors. Each year, Mary thought the beds couldn't be improved. Then Betty would develop her new design. Mary's gaze fell to the kitchen table and yesterday's newspaper. A circle surrounded a small ad for the Tanaka Garden Center.

"That's it!"

"What?"

"I bet Betty went to the Tanaka Garden Center after lunch." Mary tapped the ad. "Look. Charlene is advertising preordering spring flats. She's got all kinds listed: petunias, pansies, and other bed plants. I bet Betty saw this and got the urge to plan her spring flower beds. Who wouldn't after the winter we had?"

"Isn't it early for that?"

"Not if you're Betty and you love the design of the beds almost as much as you enjoy planting and nurturing the flowers." Mary forced a shaky smile. "If we go to the garden center, we'll learn she and Marnie Reid or Charlene Bellingham talked the afternoon away scheming and dreaming up all kinds of fresh combinations."

Henry studied her a moment. "If you say so."

"Let's check it out." Mary grabbed her purse and hurried toward the door. Maybe D.J. would call her back shortly. If not, she still had a plan: Get to the Tanaka Garden Center and see if Marnie or Charlene had any information.

Mary felt a snaking tension tighten its hold on her as Henry drove toward the garden center. Usually, she liked the short drive to Tanaka's and its location on the outskirts of Ivy Bay. The garden center was built in front of the Ivy Bay pond and was surrounded by an array of trees and plants. Charlene Bellingham, the owner, kept it stocked with an abundance of lawn ornaments and lawn fountains as well as colorful planters and an array of indoor plants next to a florist shop.

As they pulled into the parking lot, Mary sat up. "Henry, can you stop next to that car?"

"The dark blue one?"

"Yes. That looks like Betty's."

In fact, most people in town would recognize Betty's conservative vehicle. She was frugal, insisting on using a good car as long as it worked efficiently. With the way she cared for it, Mary thought it might last forever.

Henry slowed near the car, and Mary scrambled to unhook her seat belt and open the door.

"Mary." His voice trailed her, but she ignored him. She heard his door open and close but couldn't pull her gaze from the vehicle in front of her.

That was Betty's car. She had to see if Betty was in it. What if the kidnapper had made the call and then left her in the car? That couldn't be possible, but maybe Betty had left a clue.

The sedan sat to the side of the parking lot under a large maple. Had someone forced her to that spot?

Mary hurried the few steps to the car, her phone clutched in her hand. Just because Betty said she was safe didn't mean the words were true. Mary had to see what was in the car, yet something kept her from taking the final step. What would she find?

She took a deep breath and then exhaled quickly. Gathering her courage, she peeked in the front window. The seat was empty. Betty wasn't there.

She moved to the side and looked in the backseat.

Betty wasn't there either. Mary's knees quaked, and a hand slid under her arm to steady her. She sagged against Henry. "I know it's silly, but I wanted her to be here. Even if she was hurt, we could help her."

He stroked her arm as he supported her. "I know. We'll find her."

Mary nodded and pushed back to a standing position. "I'll call Chief McArthur." Everything in her itched to open the car door and dig through it for any clue, but she knew she shouldn't. She needed to leave that for the police and their experts. "Do you mind waiting to see if they find anything?"

"Of course we'll wait." Henry adjusted his sunglasses. "I'm glad we found her car."

"Me too."

They were a step closer but still so far away from finding Betty. It felt like a hollow victory. Mary hoped the kidnapper had made a mistake and left a clue behind. If not, maybe Charlene or Marnie saw something. Though if they had, wouldn't they have called the police already?

Mary rubbed her forehead as she dialed the chief. "I've found Betty's car." She relayed the location, then ended the call. She looked at Henry. "They'll be here shortly."

Neither of them said anything as they waited. A bird sang a late-morning song from the branches of the tree. An early mating call in the warm sun? A sound that would normally make her smile just made her miss Betty.

Henry moved toward the trunk of the car. "It doesn't hurt to check the outside of the car while we wait, right?"

Mary joined Henry in a walk around the car. Nothing looked amiss. Instead, it appeared Betty had parked the car and walked away.

A red car pulled into the parking lot, but it moved closer to the building.

She returned her attention to Betty's car. As she rounded the back of the vehicle to the driver's side door, she noticed the door seemed cracked. She reached into her pockets for gloves and pulled them on.

"Mary?" Henry's voice held a note of caution.

"The door's open. How could I miss that?" She edged closer, her fingers itching to open the door and explore the inside. She knew she shouldn't touch the car, but with gloves on, she wouldn't tamper with any fingerprints. She paused but didn't hear any sirens, so she eased the door open and bent to look in the interior.

Part of her prayed there would be something, anything that would indicate what had happened. But a glance revealed nothing. Absolutely nothing.

The inside of the car was as neat as Betty kept the house. Mary leaned in to look in the backseat and still didn't see anything. The only good thing about Betty keeping her vehicle so clean was that anything out of place would be more obvious. Mary longed to climb in and dig through every square inch of the interior but knew she couldn't without interfering with any evidence that might be inside. Would a defense attorney have a heyday with her opening the door? Maybe, but she was willing to risk that to find Betty. If only there was a clear clue or indication what had happened, but she couldn't see anything.

A car turned into the parking lot and skidded to a stop next to the vehicle. Mary stood, then leaned into Henry as Chief McArthur climbed out of his squad car and another officer climbed out of the passenger side. The chief stretched his long frame as he stood, watching Mary with an intelligent gaze.

"Mary Fisher, tell me you didn't climb around inside that vehicle. You of all people know better."

Henry straightened, and she could sense him tense. "She didn't do anything. I can vouch for that."

Mary sighed. "The door was open, and I made sure I had gloves on before I touched anything."

"I guess I should be grateful for small miracles." The chief cocked an eyebrow at her.

The newcomer grabbed a case from the backseat, slammed the door, and walked toward them. He stopped next to the chief. "Where do you want me to start?"

The chief looked at the car. "The driver's side." He pulled a pair of vinyl gloves from his coat pocket. "This is Don Laux, a tech we work with on evidence-heavy cases like this. He'll search Betty's car for evidence."

Mary and the short, serious man shook hands. He pushed his glasses up his nose and turned to the car. "If you'll step to the side, I'll take a quick look while I wait for Bobby."

"Why wait for Deputy Wadell?"

"He'll take the photos we'll need if this goes to court." The tech didn't wait for anything else but settled next to the car, opening his case and pulling on gloves.

A second vehicle tore into the parking lot, spitting gravel as it slid to a stop next to the chief's car. The deputy bounded from his car, a camera at the ready. "Where do you want me to start?" Then he stopped and looked at the tech where he squatted next to the car. "Who's he?"

Chief McArthur shook his head. "Bobby, you remember Don Laux, a tech with the Boston PD. He's on loan for this case. Take a couple of framing shots, location of the car to the building, street. Then we'll get shots of the interior."

Deputy Wadell made quick, methodical work of snapping a series of photos. "Digital is wonderful. Don't have to worry about how many pictures I shoot. Take a ton and then whittle down to the ones that matter." He moved toward the interior and crouched next to the car. As he took photos, he kept chattering, something that seemed out of character for the usually businesslike deputy. He was always nice but focused on his job and duties rather than talk. What was going on with the deputy?

Mary watched him another minute. "Did you see Betty at the diner yesterday?"

Deputy Wadell stopped shooting pictures and looked at her with a frown. "I forgot about that. I bumped into her—like I run into people everywhere I go. Why?"

Mary worried her lower lip between her teeth a moment. How could he have forgotten? "Someone mentioned seeing you with her. Did she mention anything about her plans?"

He shook his head. "I would have remembered that. It was the normal hello/good-bye kind of thing."

He returned to his clicking, effectively ending the conversation. At this rate, he'd fill the camera's memory card with photos of Betty's car.

Was he telling the truth about their conversation? She couldn't tell, and that bothered her. This mystery had her in knots, thinking things she normally wouldn't entertain.

As soon as Deputy Wadell stepped back from the car to move to the backseat, Chief McArthur moved to the passenger's door. The tech worked from the driver's side, and both men used deliberate and focused movements. Mary took comfort watching them. They knew what they were doing.

"Did you notice anything, Mary?" Chief McArthur glanced at her as he worked.

She shook her head. "I really didn't dig through her car. As you can tell, Betty keeps her car clean, so I didn't see anything."

"I can't picture Betty crawling around to clean under her seats."

"No, but she gets it detailed periodically." Mary watched the tech systematically examine the car. When he pulled out tape to collect samples, she knew he was being exceptionally thorough, and she was grateful.

Chief McArthur ran his hand along the point where the driver's and passenger's seats connected and came up with a slip of paper he examined. "*Hmm.* A receipt from Sam's Seafood." The tech held out a baggie, and the chief slipped the receipt inside. Then he sealed the baggie and handed it to Mary. "Did Betty eat there on Monday?"

Mary glanced at the receipt. "Betty likes meeting friends there." She shrugged before handing it back. "I suppose it's hers."

"Has she mentioned going there recently?"

"No." But that didn't mean she hadn't. After all, Mary hadn't known she was meeting D.J., and Sam's was one of Betty's favorite spots. "Do you mind if I take a photo of the receipt?"

Chief McArthur looked at the receipt one more time, then handed it back. "Okay, but if it triggers any thoughts later, let me know."

"I will." As Mary took a photo of the receipt with her phone, she wondered if she was wasting effort, but this way, she'd have her own copy to review. The receipt was dated Monday. After she handed the bagged receipt back to the chief, she tried to remember if Betty had mentioned eating at Sam's, but nothing came to mind.

"We'll be here awhile processing the car, Mary."

"Okay. Will you let me know when you're done?"

The chief looked at her, at first seemingly put out, until compassion filled his gaze. "Stay close to your phone."

"I will."

EIGHT

After the chief turned back to the car, Mary pulled out her phone and tried D.J. again. This time, there was no answer. With a grunt, she thrust the phone back in her purse. What could she do while waiting to hear from him? Her gaze traveled the parking lot and stopped on the buildings. "Want to check out the garden center with me?"

Henry turned from watching the police while he leaned against the hood of his vintage car. "Sure."

"Maybe Charlene or Marnie talked to Betty." Surely someone had.

Henry stepped toward her and slipped a hand under her elbow, guiding her across the parking lot. Since it was after ten thirty, the sign on the door had been flipped to Open. As they reached the door, it opened toward them, an electronic ding announcing their presence. Mary startled as the man from the grocery store and diner walked out of the store.

What was he doing here? Had he followed her? It couldn't be coincidence that he kept showing up in the same places she had visited over the last hours.

She took a deep breath and pushed the thoughts away. It seemed odd she'd never talked to the man before today, but there was a thin line between paranoia and vigilance. Perhaps it was only a coincidence their paths had intersected so often. After all, he hadn't come near Betty's car, not even to ask what was happening. Police converging on an abandoned car was the type of event that would attract attention.

The man moved toward his vehicle without a glance toward her. He had a bag in his hand, so he'd bought something. Maybe she really was acting paranoid.

"What was that about?" Henry watched her, curiosity tinging his tone.

"Do you know that man?"

"No. He looks like a guy who's joined a group I take out fishing every month or so. But I'm not sure."

"I haven't seen him before today. Now I've run into him three times this morning."

"Huh."

"I'm curious more than anything, though he didn't want to talk when I tried to introduce myself at the diner." Mary looked around the quiet shop. "Where's Charlene? She must have helped that man. Maybe she can tell me who he is."

"I'll be with you in just a minute." Charlene's bright voice came from around the corner.

A minute later, Charlene came around the corner, her medium-length graying hair pulled back by the usual lavender bandanna. "Sorry to keep you waiting. I was elbow deep arranging plants in a planter." Charlene's smile slipped as she looked at Mary. "I couldn't believe what happened to Betty when I saw the newspaper. Have you found her yet?" She hurried around the counter, brushing her hands on her jeans, and then took Mary's hands. "I've been just sick since I heard. What in the world is happening to our community?"

"I don't know." Mary cleared her throat as she returned Charlene's squeeze.

"What can I do for you?"

Mary pulled her shoulders back before her emotions overcame her. "Henry and I are here because we noticed Betty's car was in the parking lot."

"Is that her car?" Charlene looked toward the sliding-glass doors, as if scanning the parking lot. "When I left last night, I wondered whose car that was. I assumed whoever had left it would come back for it." She squinted through the window. "Good heavens…are those police cars?"

"Yes. I called them once I realized it was Betty's car. Charlene, do you remember what Betty came here for?"

"Sorry, Mary, but I have no idea."

"She didn't mention what she was looking for? Was she just browsing?"

"No, she never came in. Marnie didn't mention seeing her either when we were talking earlier."

"Of course." Mary was quiet for a moment. Then, even though she knew the answer, she decided to try again. "You're sure she didn't come in to talk about her plans for the garden?"

Charlene shook her head confidently. "I wish I could be more help."

Mary looked at Henry, who shrugged. This must mean whoever had taken Betty had followed her from the diner to the garden center and abducted her before she'd entered the building. The trail ended here.

But who would do such a thing? Who would follow Betty and pull her from her car before she even came in? Her car had been parked farther from the door than Mary would have expected, especially if the store was slow, a decision likely made under duress.

As if reading her thoughts, Henry chimed in. "And you didn't notice any unusual activity in the parking lot?"

Charlene looked at Henry. "Not at all. But I was organizing the store for the spring flower sales, so I didn't spend much time looking out the windows." Charlene turned her attention to Mary. "You should call Marnie. One of her kids is sick today, so you can reach her at home."

"Thanks, I will. If you think of anything…"

"I'll call that minute."

Mary turned toward the door, but a thought occurred to her. "Oh, one question about the man who was in here right before us."

"Jonathan Anderson? What about him?"

"Do you mind telling me what he bought?"

"Rose insect killer. He said the mites did a number on his bushes last year. Something about getting a head start while he had the chance. I guess what he bought yesterday didn't look right when he got to his cabin."

Jonathan had been here yesterday too? "Do you happen to know where his cabin is?"

"I don't know exactly where, but he owns a small cottage outside of town. He's mentioned that it's his place to escape from the big city when he can. He seems to be a pretty avid gardener."

"Do you know what he does in Boston?"

Charlene shrugged. "He's a professor at one of the universities. Maybe MIT. He told me once he has the cottage so he can get away from the students occasionally."

"Thanks, Charlene." Mary reached out and squeezed her hand. "You've been so helpful."

"Please let me know if you have any more questions. Let me give you Marnie's number." Charlene wrote it on a piece of paper, then bid good-bye to Henry and Mary.

Henry pushed the door open for Mary. The metallic ding followed them, and Mary grabbed her phone from her purse and entered Marnie's home number. "Might as well call Marnie now, in case she knows something."

"Good plan," Henry agreed.

It took a quick call to learn Marnie hadn't talked to Betty or seen anything unusual in the parking lot either. She'd been busy planning the details for a couple of spring weddings.

Mary looked at Henry as she returned her phone to her purse, frustration threatening to overtake her. She took a deep breath as they approached the police vehicle that still waited next to Betty's car.

Chief McArthur greeted them. "Learn anything interesting?"

"Just that Betty never made it into the store."

"So she was taken here." The chief looked across the parking lot, then toward the street. "I guess that makes sense. The store is remote and wouldn't have much traffic this time of year. I'll follow up with Charlene after we finish processing the car."

"Learn anything so far?"

"Not yet." He held up a hand. "And we haven't received the ransom demand yet. I don't know why. But we still have the Boston Police tech stationed at Eleanor's."

Mary looked around. "Where did Deputy Wadell go?"

"To check on things at the station." Mary stilled as his gaze captured her attention. "We're working hard, Mary."

She nodded. "I guess we'll keep looking."

"I've got one thing for you." The chief turned and grabbed something from the driver's seat. It was a phone inside a plastic baggie. "Does this look familiar?"

Mary studied it without grabbing the phone. "It looks like Betty's."

The chief powered it up. "Does this help?"

"May I?" Mary reached for it.

The chief handed it to her, and she tried to slide the screen. "The plastic is getting in the way, but slide it on and you'll see a picture of Betty's flower beds from last summer." She handed it back. "I guess GPS won't help us find her now either."

"No. Keep your phone on and close by." The chief's phone rang, and he pulled it out. A moment later, he was moving toward his car, an intent expression on his face. "We'll be there in a minute." He hung up and turned to Mary. "Ransom call. You might want to follow me to Eleanor's."

"Let's go," Henry said. He was already climbing into his car. By the time she sat down and fastened her seat belt, he was headed out of the parking lot, following the chief as he hurried down the road toward Eleanor's.

NINE

◆◆◆

When they reached Eleanor's home, Mary hurried out of the car and up the sidewalk. She was only a step behind Chief McArthur as he knocked. Henry followed close behind.

Eleanor opened the door; tight lines radiating around her eyes and lips. "He wants fifty thousand dollars. *Fifty thousand dollars.* Tomorrow morning." She waved a hand in the air, and Mary noticed she held her cell phone. "Like I can snap my fingers and get that kind of cash."

Chief McArthur nodded and hurried toward the dining room where the technician fiddled with the equipment.

"Oh, Eleanor, I'm so sorry. Are you all right?" Mary squeezed Eleanor's arm.

Eleanor forced a pained smile. "No better than you, Mary, I'm sure." She sighed. "I called the bank. They understand the situation and are working to collect the cash now. Then they have to do something with listing the numbers so they can identify the bills when the kidnapper uses them. Plus something about adding dye packs to try to catch him the moment he opens the ransom bag." She rubbed her forehead. "I just want this nightmare over and Betty back here with us."

"We both do." Mary took Eleanor's hand in hers. "I don't have much money, Eleanor, but I'll contribute what I can. I can put another mortgage on the bookshop."

"I can find some cash too," Henry said.

Eleanor shook her head. "No. It's only money, Mary. Betty is much more important to me than fifty thousand dollars." She glanced at the phone as if remembering she held it. "He'll call with drop-off instructions in the morning. Don't kidnappers want their money fast? I don't understand these delays."

Eleanor's words echoed Mary's thoughts. The longer the kidnapper strung them along, the longer Betty was gone and the more chance something would happen to her sister. Why was he delaying? Could it mean he was unprepared? That this was a spontaneous opportunity he'd taken? Yet he'd still known who to call with the demands.

Henry stood behind Mary. "When does the kidnapper want the money?"

"Sometime tomorrow morning. He didn't give us a time yet." Eleanor's phone rang, and she glanced at the screen. "It's the bank." She stepped into the living room, and Mary looked over toward the dining room. The chief, who was talking intently to the tech, picked up a headset.

Mary tried to imagine where Betty was. As her mind spiraled through a myriad of options, she felt a physical pain as she realized she didn't know *how* Betty was. Then she realized she shouldn't have to imagine her sister's current situation. If the kidnapper wanted money, he had to prove Betty was still alive. She'd read enough novels about kidnapping to know that was true.

Chief McArthur walked toward Mary.

"Do you think we can get proof of life?" she asked him.

"We can ask for it. It's definitely something to coach Eleanor to ask for the next time the kidnapper calls."

"Would you? I'd feel better knowing Betty was still okay."

"Believe that, Mary." The chief's eyes were intense as he studied her. "We don't have any reason to think that's changed, and we'll ask for proof."

"Thank you."

"Glad to do it for you." The technician called him over. "Sorry I have to go, but I'll keep you updated on any developments."

As he walked away, Mary was grateful for his care with the investigation. And with her.

Henry leaned against the wall. "Where to?"

Mary's stomach grumbled, and she glanced at her watch. It was after one. No wonder she was hungry. "Home. I'll make a quick lunch while trying Jean and D.J. again."

Somehow Mary had to get through to D.J. She considered asking the chief to find him, but the chief needed to stay close for any more calls from the kidnapper. Besides, there was no reason at this point to send the police to D.J.'s door.

A few minutes later, she stood in her kitchen, staring at the calendar while Henry made sandwiches. Henry settled at the table with a glass of iced tea and a sandwich. As Mary scanned backward on the calendar, she stopped on an entry a few days earlier. Betty had made a note to return a call from D.J. There wasn't more to the note, but why hadn't Betty mentioned the call to her? Or the fact they planned to meet for lunch? Usually that was the kind of information Betty would share easily and readily as they had dinner together.

It simply didn't make sense that Betty would keep the information to herself.

What had the two of them been up to? At the least, Betty would have mentioned it because D.J. was family. But she hadn't. That was what made the whole situation so odd.

After another call to D.J.'s apartment went unanswered, Mary pulled up Jean's number and called her cousin again. This time, Jean answered on the third ring.

"Mary. I was just about to return your call. Everything okay? You need to reach D.J.?" Jean's voice held a curious note.

"I have bad news. Betty was kidnapped last night." After Jean finished exclaiming and demanding to know every detail, Mary continued. "One of the last people she saw was D.J. Do you know how I can reach him?"

Silence was all Mary heard for a minute before Jean spoke. "Why?"

"Because we need to re-create where Betty went and who she saw. We received a ransom call a little while ago."

"I haven't talked to D.J. for a few days. His classes at MIT are keeping him so busy. I suppose they should, considering the ridiculous amount they charge for tuition. There are days I wonder if it can possibly be worth it." She sighed. "But that's not important right now. What number are you using?"

Mary rattled off the number she'd found.

"That's the right number. Every once in a while, it can be hard to reach D.J. on the landline, so let me give you his cell number." Jean dictated the number, and Mary read it back to her. "Yes, that's it."

"Thanks, Jean. And if you hear from D.J., please have him call me."

"Sure. Is there anything else I can do?"

"You can pray."

"You know I will. Without ceasing."

"Thanks, Jean. Love you."

"Love you too, Mary."

Mary tried the new number but still didn't get an answer and hung up without leaving a message. She looked at Henry. "So you really don't mind the drive?"

"Not at all. I've got a full tank of gas."

She grabbed two bottles of water from the fridge. "Can I get you anything else?"

Henry accepted one of the bottles. "This is great. Are you going to eat your sandwich?"

Mary picked it up and took a bite, chewing idly. The food had no taste, but she knew she had to eat to stay focused and alert. When she finished her meal, she put the plate in the dishwasher and turned to Henry, who had been reading the paper. "Ready?"

"Yes, ma'am."

She grabbed a couple of granola bars from the cabinet and slipped them into her purse, then followed Henry to the front porch. Gus tried to slip out behind her, but she coaxed him back inside before locking the door. "Sorry, buddy. I know you want to find her too. But you've got to keep watch here."

After they were in Henry's car, he turned to her and asked, "Where to?"

"Quincy, please."

"Why does this cousin live in Quincy?"

Mary shook her head as Henry eased onto the road, heading out of Ivy Bay. "I'm not sure. He came back in January to restart his degree at MIT. I guess he didn't want to live in Boston proper. Or maybe he found an apartment he could more easily afford away from campus and Boston."

As Henry drove, Mary pulled out a slim notebook and jotted a few notes. When she finished, the page still had a depressing amount of white space considering everyone she'd talked to. From Margie, she'd learned Betty had gone to the diner. And Nicole had told her Betty had met D.J. Then an unknown man talked with D.J. at the diner. But that wasn't much to go on. Betty's car was at the garden center, but there weren't any real clues pointing to where she'd gone next or who had taken her. And—although Mary had no idea how this was relevant—Dr. Anderson kept showing up, and she couldn't figure out why.

She had also noted the kidnapper wanted fifty thousand dollars but wasn't in a hurry to collect the ransom.

She closed the notebook and prayed D.J. would be home when they arrived. Maybe he could shed more light on the situation.

Her phone rang, and she scrambled through her purse for it. "Hello?"

"Is this Mary?"

"Yes, D.J., thanks for calling me back." Mary took a deep breath to steady a voice that suddenly shook. She'd begun to worry she wouldn't reach him, yet he was one of her last links to Betty.

"Mom called and said you're trying to reach me. She made it sound serious." He chuckled in an awkward way. "Here I am."

"Are you at your apartment?"

"Yes, ma'am, I'm here. What's up?"

"Is it okay if I stop by in a few minutes?"

"Is this about Betty? Mom mentioned she was kidnapped. Unbelievable." There was a pause. "You're welcome to come over, if you think that's best. Otherwise we can talk now."

"We're almost there. If traffic cooperates, we'll arrive in about ten minutes, okay?"

"Sure, see you then."

Mary prayed that D.J. would have information, any information that would help.

TEN

D.J.'s apartment complex was set off the road, with a parking lot fronting the multistory brick buildings. While nice, there was nothing spectacular about the high-rise.

"His apartment is on the fifth floor," Mary said.

Henry parked in a parking spot spray-painted for visitors. He slid from the car and came around to open her door. "Glad he's home."

"Me too. Thanks for driving."

"You know I always enjoy time with you."

Mary followed him to the sidewalk, and they walked side by side. She shivered as a breeze snaked between her coat and scarf to her neck. She waited as Henry opened the front door. Then he led the way to the elevator and eventually D.J.'s door. She used the doorbell, the sound loud and echoing in the hallway. A minute later, a voice called through the door.

D.J. opened the door, his dark hair sticking out in all directions as if he'd still been in bed, but his roommate had told her he wasn't home. "Hi, Mary. Good to see you."

"You too, D.J." She hugged him, then gestured to Henry. "This is my friend Henry."

"Nice to meet you," D.J. said, and the two men shook hands.

D.J. stepped back, giving them space to come in. "I thought I'd heard you wrong on the message. Then Mom called. Why was Betty kidnapped? We're talking about your sister, right? How is something like that even possible?"

Mary shook her head as she joined him in the living room. It didn't make sense. And no one understood how it could happen.

"Sorry we're not the best housekeepers. Spring break has us going in lots of different directions." D.J. shrugged. "I've barely seen Connor this week. He's got a lot going on."

Mary smiled as she remembered when her son's first apartment looked much like this one. She wanted to say it was a season that would pass but had a feeling Jean would care more about it than D.J. "We'll be fine on the couch."

Henry harrumphed as he moved a pile of unopened mail and newspapers and placed it on top of the stack of teetering pizza boxes.

"Can I get you something to drink?" D.J. walked to his small kitchen and opened the refrigerator. "I've got Gatorade, milk, Mountain Dew...."

Mary and Henry exchanged an amused glance at the distinctly bachelor choices. "Water is fine. Thanks."

"Water for two, coming up."

Mary took in his apartment. A scratched coffee table stood between a russet leather couch and a battered navy chair. Discarded pizza boxes and empty soda and water bottles were piled on top of the table, while the TV was on but muted. A pillow and blanket had slid off the couch as if disturbed when D.J. got up to answer the door.

Henry slipped off his coat and placed it on the couch as if to protect her from grime. "Your seat, madam."

"Henry." It felt good to laugh at his chivalrous action. "I'm glad you're with me today." His wink was answer enough.

D.J. returned with two glasses of water. Then he sank onto the edge of an overstuffed chair that had seen better days. The old MIT sweatshirt thrown over the edge of it looked well worn too, as though it was from his first day at the school. "So what happened?"

"Betty called Eleanor last night. Told her she'd been kidnapped. Then the kidnapper called an hour ago and made his demand."

D.J. shook his head as if unable to process the information. She knew how he felt. "That's terrible. But why come here?"

"Because the only person I haven't talked to yet who I know saw her yesterday is you."

Well, and the kidnapper. A door slammed shut down the hall, and Mary jumped.

"Sorry." D.J. flushed and looked at the ground. "My roommate, Connor. He doesn't really know how to be quiet. It's taken a little getting used to." D.J. was an only child, so Mary could imagine a loud roommate would require an adjustment.

"I'm headed out." A skinny, tall young man who resembled a scarecrow in a parka came to a stop. "Oh. Sorry. I didn't know we had visitors."

"Mary, my mom's cousin, and her friend Henry," D.J. said. Henry turned to D.J.'s roommate and extended his hand.

The roommate gave a halfhearted shake and peered through wire-rimmed glasses that made him look a bit like Clark Kent. "What's going on?"

Mary frowned at the abrupt young man, but D.J. spoke up. "It's crazy, but Mary's sister, Betty, has been kidnapped. Mary's here to talk to me about it."

The roommate looked surprised but shrugged it off. "Kidnapping? I thought that only happened in movies." He grabbed a lacrosse stick from a corner by the large-screen TV. "I'm off to practice. See ya sometime later." He tapped the edge of the stick against the floor, then left without another glance.

"Sorry about that. Connor doesn't have very good social skills. He's the only child of the sort of family that has a summer beach house, so..." D.J. rolled his eyes, but then his face fell and he looked sheepish. "His parents are getting a divorce, and I think it's kind of wrecked him."

Mary felt bad for the young man but didn't appreciate his rude behavior. "That's too bad. Can you fill me in on why you and Betty had lunch?"

D.J.'s green eyes glazed as if he couldn't quite understand the question. "I needed to talk to Betty."

"About...?"

He shrugged and settled deeper into the navy chair. "Well, uh...I've been kicking around this idea for a business. It's one of the reasons I came back to school. It's harder to get started than I'd thought. That diploma matters an awful lot to people." He ran his fingers through his hair, leaving the dark hair standing up in all directions.

"It does make a difference."

"I wanted to be the next Bill Gates or Steve Jobs. Show you can successfully innovate without all that time in school. But that didn't happen." He shrugged. "Mom says I wasted a year. Maybe she's right. I need a little more background that I'll get at MIT before I can work the magic I can see in my mind. So I'm back to finish the degree and develop my ideas. MIT has a great incubator program, and I want to take full advantage of it. But, well"—D.J. shifted and looked sheepish—"I'll need financial backing to make it work. It made sense to meet with Betty, see what she thought about my project, if she'd be interested in investing. So she listened to my ideas and gave me advice and feedback."

"On school?"

"Yeah, and on my business ideas. She has a lot of good advice. All those years watching Edward build his business rubbed off."

Mary sat back and considered. It made sense. Betty was a savvy, intelligent woman with significant capital at her disposal. "I'm surprised she didn't mention your appointment to me."

D.J. flushed and looked away. "I sort of . . . asked her not to. Sorry, Mary. But it was scary enough asking her to listen. I didn't need the pressure of more people asking how my plans were developing. Besides, you know books, but this is electronics and technology. I didn't want to waste your time."

Mary didn't know whether to laugh or be offended. Betty wasn't exactly tech savvy either.

He must have seen something in her expression because he held his hands up. "I just mean that I know how busy you are and didn't want to waste your time on something that might be stupid. Besides, I figured you need to keep investing in your store, not take a risk on me."

She smiled reassuringly. "It's okay, D.J. I understand. How long did you stay at the diner?"

He frowned and his brows lowered. "I don't know…maybe an hour? Not more than that. Seems like I got back before two, and we met about eleven thirty."

That fit roughly with the time frame. Why had the kidnapper waited to call until after nine o'clock that night?

Henry cleared his throat, and she pulled her attention back to the moment. "Was your meeting helpful?"

"Sure. Betty asked great questions and was really supportive. She got me thinking about different approaches we could take and encouraged me to stay with my classes. She even encouraged me to take a few business classes. She said an entrepreneur needed to understand accounting and business strategy." He shrugged. "I'm not convinced about that, but maybe I'll check with my adviser after spring break. See if I can add classes to my course load."

"What's your idea, D.J.?" Henry's question set D.J. off on a conversation that became largely one-sided as he talked about a gadget and gizmo he'd designed that could make computers process even faster than they already did. Mary listened with one part of her brain while considering what he'd said in the context of what she already knew.

When D.J. finally paused, Mary asked, "Did Betty say where she was headed after your meeting?"

He shook his head. "No."

"You're sure?" Henry leaned forward, his focus riveted on D.J.

"Yeah." He didn't hesitate. "We argued over who would pay, though I let her win. Betty's generous, and money's tight for this college student." His cheeks colored a bit as he admitted that. "After she paid, we left the diner and headed to our cars."

Mary considered his response. It certainly fit with what she'd expect Betty to do. "Did you notice anyone following her?"

D.J. frowned at the question. "You think someone followed her from the diner?"

"That's what I think, yes."

"But *why* would someone do that? Why kidnap Betty?" D.J. asked.

Mary sighed. "For money, of course."

"But Betty has money. She can't pay her own ransom."

"That's true." Mary paused until D.J. met her gaze. "But Eleanor has more. Maybe the kidnapper knew about Eleanor's wealth and considered her an easier target." Mary checked her cell phone again. No missed calls from the chief. She set her phone on top of the coffee table, where a pile of schoolwork and textbooks sat. A syllabus rested on top. "Studying during spring break?"

"Yeah." He pointed to the syllabus. "That class is so challenging. I don't think I've ever studied as hard for a B in my life." D.J. grinned ruefully. "The professor's good. It's too bad half of what he says is unintelligible."

Mary laughed until she noted the professor's name on the syllabus. "Wait. Is your professor Jonathan Anderson?"

ELEVEN

D.J. looked surprised at Mary's reaction. "Yeah. He's an expert in the field. Guess you have to be to teach at MIT. Why? Do you know him?"

D.J.'s question caught Mary off guard. Did she know Dr. Anderson? No, not before today when he suddenly appeared everywhere she went. Now she needed to know more about him so she could understand why he kept intersecting her path as it related to Betty's kidnapping.

"I don't know him." She looked at D.J., who frowned as if he were confused at her interest.

"Can you tell us what his class is about?" Henry asked, once again reading Mary's mind.

"Sure. He calls it computational and systems biology." At Mary's blank look, D.J. grinned. "It's really about how different systems function within biology and computers. I'd never thought about how the two could overlap. It took him about two classes to define the topic. After a slow start, it's been pretty interesting." D.J. continued to talk about how this class was similar to his other tech classes, how they expanded the way he thought about technology. "It's pretty incredible to think I'm studying under professors who are pushing the envelopes of technology and research. There's such mind-blowing complexity out there. I just hope someday it comes together so I can use it in my job."

D.J.'s passion caught Mary's interest, but she didn't want to lose focus on why she was there. "I'm glad you're learning so much, D.J. It seems like your decision to return to school was a good one. Could I ask another question about your professor?" Mary tapped the syllabus.

"Yeah?"

"What does he look like?"

D.J. shrugged. "He's average height, middle-aged. Not too tall or too short. Not too thin or too big. Just kind of average with thinning hair. Drives a red car."

That description matched the man she'd run into numerous times that morning. "I ran into him this morning in Ivy Bay."

"I'm not surprised. He's mentioned owning a cottage near there. He talks about how he likes to escape to Ivy Bay. He might teach in Boston, but I get the sense he doesn't like the city. In fact, I saw him at the diner as I left with Betty."

So Jonathan Anderson was the one Nicole had seen talking with D.J. yesterday. The way he intersected in so many ways with Betty's kidnapping made him suspicious to Mary. "Do you remember if Dr. Anderson left the diner when you did?"

He thought for a moment. "I don't think so, but I really don't know." D.J. stood. "I'll ask my roommate if he remembers. He stopped by too."

"He did?" So maybe it was Connor who Nicole saw talking to D.J. Why did it seem like everyone had ended up at the diner yesterday? Mary supposed that wasn't unusual—it was one of the most popular meeting spots in Ivy Bay.

The shrill tone of her phone pulled Mary from her thoughts. "Sorry, D.J. If you don't mind, this could be about Betty."

"Of course."

She looked at her phone and saw Eleanor's name on the caller ID. "Hi, Eleanor. Any news?"

"The kidnapper just called again. I'm beginning to think he's the most disorganized kidnapper in history. I asked for proof of life like Chief McArthur suggested."

Mary stood, then walked into the tiny galley kitchen. "Is he getting it?"

"He'd better, because I insisted I was working on the money but wouldn't deliver it until I knew Betty was okay. He hung up after that." She paused. "Did I do the right thing, Mary?"

Mary nodded, then voiced her agreement. "Yes. We have to know Betty's okay."

"You'll be glad to know my banker's working hard on the money side. He still needs some time to mark the bills, but then all we're waiting on is proof of life. After that, I'll have to deliver the money if the kidnapper can get organized enough to tell me where."

"Thank you for doing all of this, Eleanor."

"Of course. Well, I'd better go."

Eleanor hung up, and Mary stood in the kitchen, ignoring the piled-up dishes in D.J.'s sink as she looked out the window. A bird sat in a tree that extended empty branches to the sky. That was how she felt. Stripped bare as she prayed God would protect Betty. All she could extend were arms empty of anything of value. Still, she knew God heard and cared. She had to take comfort in that knowledge as she waited for Betty to come home.

"Everything okay?" At Henry's words, she turned away from the window.

"Eleanor heard from the kidnapper again."

"That's good?"

"I hope so. Eleanor asked for proof of life." She shook her head as she studied Henry. "I never thought I'd use those words in connection with Betty."

Henry rubbed her arms. "Glad we'll know she's okay."

"Me too." She stepped away and headed back into the living room. "We need to return to Ivy Bay."

"Anything I can do?" D.J. studied her as if he didn't really want an answer. That was okay. She was tired of the question anyway.

"I'll let you know if there is. Thanks."

He mumbled something as she left the apartment, Henry a half step behind her.

"Should we head back to Eleanor's?"

"I think so, yes." She wanted to hear recordings of the calls, if the chief would let her, and then decide what to do. She rubbed her temples, pushing back the tension that threatened to hold her in its grip. "I keep wondering why the kidnapper asked for that amount of money."

"*Hmm?*" Henry glanced at her before turning his attention back to the road.

"Well, why fifty thousand dollars? Why not one hundred thousand dollars? Or less? The kidnapper has a reason he asked for that sum."

Could she figure out who had grabbed Betty if she looked into who needed fifty thousand dollars? She needed something she could research—maybe this was it. If she built a list of people who knew Eleanor and Betty and needed money, perhaps she could identify a few suspects.

"Maybe he has debts to pay." Henry tapped the steering wheel.

"Or something he wants to buy." The possibilities were limitless for who would want that amount of money. "Until we know who it is, I can't understand why he did this."

"He needs money."

"Sure, but lots of people need money. Doesn't mean they resort to kidnapping to get it."

Henry changed lanes, then slowed for a light. "So do we start a list of people with money woes?"

"That's what I'm thinking. Of course, we're assuming the kidnapper is someone we know, which might not necessarily be true. But it's a good first step." Mary sighed as she looked out the window at the familiar Massachusetts scenery as they headed back to Ivy Bay.

"It seems more likely the kidnapper is someone who knows Betty and Eleanor, versus a total stranger."

Mary nodded. She considered who she might know with financial difficulties, and then it dawned on her. Deputy Wadell appeared to be in the midst of money trouble.

But would he kidnap Betty to solve his financial woes?

TWELVE

—◆◆—

Mary's phone rang, and she dug it out of her purse, then looked at the caller ID. "Hi, Evan."

"Hello, Aunt Mary. Where are you?"

"On the road back to Ivy Bay."

"Aunt Eleanor just let me know they've received the ransom demand." Evan's words came in quick bursts. "Did you know he's asking for fifty thousand dollars? How am I supposed to find that kind of money in twenty-four hours?"

"Yes, I heard. You don't need to find the money. I'm sure Eleanor told you she's working on it."

"I know, but she shouldn't have to. Nobody should have to, Aunt Mary." A few ragged breaths were all she heard. "I feel so helpless."

"I do too."

Silence settled between them for a moment before Evan spoke again. "Well, you should see all the people who want to organize a search. You wouldn't believe how many people have called asking how they can help. My phone hasn't stopped ringing. What should I tell them?"

"Have you talked with Margie at church? She talked about compiling a list of people who wanted to help."

"I'll do that. We aren't the only ones who feel like we have to do something."

Mary knew what he meant. "It might be time to start a search, but Chief McArthur will have to make the final call. Will you be sure to coordinate with him, since he'll have thoughts on where a search should be conducted? He and Deputy Wadell have asked that we stay out of the way of police efforts. And if you talk to Pastor Miles, can you let me know what he says?"

"Of course. And please keep me updated on what you learn too."

"Absolutely." Then she said, as much for herself as for her nephew, "We will find her."

After she hung up, Mary repeated that phrase to herself. She believed it even if she wasn't sure where to look. She continued to stare out the window, her thoughts a tangled web.

"We're almost back, Mary."

Henry's words pulled her from the quagmire of distracted thoughts. "Oh good."

"How about we stop at the Tea Shoppe? We can grab something to drink and then head wherever you need to go next."

The thought of one of Sophie Mershon's special blends warmed Mary. "I'd like that."

A few minutes later, they arrived in Ivy Bay, and Henry parked his car in front of the Tea Shoppe. "A tall tea?"

"That would be great."

Mary stayed in the car, keeping her trembling hands clasped in her lap. She shivered as she remembered the last time she'd stopped at the shop. It had been Sunday, and she and Betty had ordered quiche after church. Sophie had been all smiles about a new shipment filled with fresh varieties of tea she couldn't wait for them to try. Sophie had pulled canister after canister down from her shelves, and Betty and Mary had smelled the fragrant teas until they blended together. They had made plans to come back Thursday—tomorrow—for tea and scones. They'd sample as many of the new blends as Sophie had prepared and probably coax her into brewing a few more.

Mary desperately wanted to keep that appointment.

When Henry exited the store, he held a tall to-go cup in each hand. Sophie followed with a to-go box clutched in her hands. Mary pushed her door open as Henry held a cup toward her.

"Thanks, Henry." She accepted the cup and inhaled the heady aroma before setting it in a holder. Then she began to push to her feet.

"Don't get out of the car, Mary." Sophie approached the car, and her usually placid voice had a ragged edge. "I've been heartbroken since hearing about Betty." She handed the box to Mary with a small smile. "I know this isn't much, but if I were in your shoes, the last thing I would think about is food. Here's a slice of today's quiche with some salad. Enough for a light meal when you need nourishment later."

Mary smiled through a sheen of tears. "That's so thoughtful."

"It's a small way to show I care." Sophie stood in a fluid motion, revealing her years as a professional ballerina. "If there is anything else I can do—anything at all—please call. I don't care what time of day or night."

"I will."

"Even if it's providing hot drinks for those helping with the search."

"There's a search?" There was no way Evan had sufficient time, so Pastor Miles must already be working with Chief McArthur. Evan would be pleased to hear it.

"I don't know what else to call it. It started slowly, but I think they're getting organized."

"That's good to hear." Mary set the box on the dashboard, then returned her attention to her friend. "Sophie, do you remember the last time you saw Betty?"

After a pause, Sophie looked at Mary. "It must have been yesterday. I watched her leave the Black & White Diner with a young man."

"Did you recognize him?"

"No. I'd never seen him before. He seemed shorter than Henry, thin, and young."

Yep, that was D.J. Dr. Anderson wasn't old, but he certainly wasn't young.

"I'm trying to retrace Betty's steps yesterday. Did you happen to notice if anyone followed Betty from the diner?"

Sophie frowned as she worried her lower lip between her teeth. "I didn't. But that doesn't mean it didn't happen. I only saw them at a quick glance."

"Of course." Mary smiled, even as her heart ached. She was hitting the point where the tidbits she gathered began to overlap. The problem was she needed a way to jump-start a new avenue. Maybe if Chief McArthur let her listen to the ransom call she'd think of something. There was also the chance the proof of life would reveal some detail about Betty's location. And she would continue to consider who she knew with financial struggles, although that list would be hard to fully compile. Most people with money troubles kept them private. Deputy Wadell certainly hadn't intended for Mary to know about his.

Behind Henry and Sophie, Blake Bailey approached. He looked into the car. "Hi, Mary, I'm so glad to see you here. You won't believe what is happening at the ice-cream shop."

"What?"

Blake waved a hand in the air. "It seems anyone who's ever met you or Betty is determined to help find her. And they've decided the ice-cream shop should be the headquarters, something I'm more than happy to accommodate."

"Do you have room for everyone?" Henry smiled. "Sounds like it's turning into a crowd."

"I can hardly hear myself think. But it's worth it."

Mary looked at Henry, who just shrugged as if he didn't understand any more than Mary. "You're going to have to slow down, Blake."

The man got a big grin on his face. "You didn't tell her, Sophie?"

"I'd started."

Mary eased from the car, afraid she'd develop a crick in her neck if she kept looking up at Blake. "Tell me more about what's happening at your store."

"It's been the craziest thing. Folks are taking turns praying for Betty in the chapel at Grace. Margie plans to keep someone in there until Betty's home."

"That's wonderful." She paused, waiting to see what any of this had to do with the ice-cream shop.

Henry braced his elbows on the roof of his car and watched Blake. "And?"

"People want to do more. They want to do something tangible to bring Betty home." Blake took a breath and spread his hands wide. "So all day, people have talked about helping the police search. Evan just called to say he'd talked to Deputy Wadell and should have search maps soon. Pastor Miles keeps directing people our way too. We're about ready to start, and I thought you'd want to come."

"I'm really touched everybody wants to do something." But watching other people work didn't seem like the best use of her time.

"People want to see you, make sure you're okay. We love you and Betty." Blake stopped as if uncertain how she'd react to his next words. "Kaley mentioned she'd need your help too, before she could do anything."

"Do what?" Mary smiled as she remembered the young woman's determination to help.

"She's got Pipp at the store, just in case he can help us find Betty. He's a well-behaved dog, but I can't let him stay. Health-code rules."

"I understand. Earlier today Kaley did offer Pipp's assistance." It wouldn't hurt to run over to the ice-cream shop for a few minutes. Her friends were doing their best to help, and she wanted to honor their efforts. She couldn't discount the fact that they might actually find Betty. Henry met her gaze and nodded. She smiled, thankful for her stalwart friend. "We'd be glad to come. Thanks for all you're doing, Blake. I appreciate the support."

"I'll let everyone know you're on your way." He hurried across the street and down the block toward his store.

After she thanked Sophie again for her kindness, Mary followed Blake at a slower pace. She had a hard time believing it hadn't been quite twenty-four hours since she'd dropped off the new ice-cream recipe at Bailey's. Last night, the shop had been fairly empty, one or two people sipping shakes at the small wrought-iron tables. As she and Henry approached now, the store buzzed with action, full of people who paced and milled in the limited space.

Before they reached Bailey's, the front door of the ice-cream shop opened, and a few people walked out to usher Mary toward the store. She felt carried on a wave of their love and concern.

Dorothy Johnson, Jill Sanderson, and Amy Stebble were there from her prayer group. Frances Curran and Madeline Dinsdale from Betty's book club looked eager to do something. Kip and Heather Hastings, Sherry Walinski, and Matilda Bressie were just a few more of their many friends from Grace Church who waited as Mary entered the shop.

Everywhere Mary looked, she spotted more and more friends—people who loved her sister.

She was thoroughly touched and had rarely been so grateful that she'd left Boston for Ivy Bay. What a community this was. More important, they were willing to adjust their lives in a time of crisis. She'd seen them rally before but never in such a cohesive, sweeping way. She didn't try to stop the tears running down her cheeks as gratitude filled her heart.

When the hugs slowed to a trickle, she sniffed and looked around the room at the friends congregated there. "Thank you for caring so much about Betty. It means so much that you love her and are praying for her. She'll be grateful too."

As she looked at her friends, Mary wondered if they weren't right that it was time for an organized search. All her interviews and searching hadn't given her any direction on where the kidnapper held Betty. Maybe it was time to do something—to search Ivy Bay in grids and see if they could find her.

Kaley Court elbowed her way toward Mary, her big golden retriever bounding by her side on a leash. Her hair was pulled back in a wild ponytail and a thick green scarf was wrapped around her neck, emphasizing the brown in her eyes. "We're ready to get started, Mary. And if you're okay with us sending Pipp out, I need something of Betty's. Preferably clothes she wore recently."

Mary thought about it. She knew Kaley was eager to help, and she certainly didn't think Pipp would *hurt* their search efforts. "All right. I'll grab something from home."

Deputy Wadell shouldered his way through the crowd until he stood next to Kaley. He looked agitated. "Mary, I'm not sure you want to do this."

"Oh? Why not, Deputy?"

"You don't know what could happen. Someone could get hurt." He looked away, then turned back, meeting her gaze with deep pain reflected in his eyes. "What if the kidnapper gets mad?"

He had a point, and she was inclined to trust his position. However, he hadn't seemed himself since yesterday. Whatever was causing his financial worries, combined with his worry over the kidnapping, seemed to have put him off his perfect professionalism.

"Surely the kidnapper expects us to search for Betty. I can't imagine he thinks we'd stand idly by waiting for him to return her."

He met her gaze with intensity. "Okay, Mary. I'm not going to stop this, but"—he sighed so deeply it seemed to rattle him—"it's fine, I guess. Just remember that even a trained dog can't pick up a scent if Betty was moved in a vehicle."

THIRTEEN

It didn't take Mary long to run into her house, grab Betty's robe, and put it in a paper bag. She stopped at the kitchen counter out of habit to check for a message from Betty, then swallowed as she realized she wouldn't find any notes until Betty's captor released her.

The answering machine blinked a staccato flash, alerting her that many messages waited. She stopped long enough to listen to the prayers and offers of help from a collection of friends. But not one message held Betty's voice. Mary pushed away from the counter and breathed another prayer for Betty's protection. She was so grateful God knew where she was and could see Betty in these times.

After grabbing another couple of bottles of water from the refrigerator, Mary hurried through the front door to the street, where Henry waited beside his car. As he held the door for her, she slid in, holding the bottles and bag in her lap.

Once he was settled behind the wheel, he turned to her. "Are you sure you want to do this, Mary?"

As the weight of the bag settled on her, she thought of what it represented. Her friends' hope that they could find Betty and bring her home quickly and safely.

"Pipp probably won't find her." She chuckled at the image of the big dog bounding around downtown, knocking things over with his big tail. "But I don't mind trying. What if Pipp does sense something and follows her trail somewhere we don't expect?"

"It's possible."

Henry turned left onto Main Street, then slid his car into a spot in front of the bookstore. With the paper bag in hand, Mary got out of the car, and she and Henry crossed the street to the crowd that spilled out of Bailey's.

Mary froze when she noticed Jonathan Anderson standing next to Deputy Wadell on the sidewalk, flashing a paper around.

"What on earth?"

"Everything all right?" Henry walked with her across the street.

"Look who's here."

"Now I see what you mean about Dr. Anderson showing up everywhere."

She walked up to the professor. "Dr. Anderson."

He startled, then turned his attention to Mary. "Yes?"

"I introduced myself to you earlier today." At his blank look, she tried again, even though he must realize they'd overlapped at locations four times now, far too many to be a coincidence. "I'm Mary Fisher, Betty Emerson's sister."

"Oh yes. I'm so sorry about what's happened." He held up the map. "Trying to do my bit to help find her."

She looked at Deputy Wadell and quirked an eyebrow. *Why was Dr. Anderson advising the police?* The deputy just shrugged. She turned back to Dr. Anderson. "What do you have there?"

"A map of the town divided into segments." He extended it toward her.

She accepted it and saw it was exactly what the professor had said. A map of Ivy Bay broken into grids with a pen. She was a little surprised the grids didn't reach all the way to the garden center. "That was kind of you to do this."

"It seemed a useful way to use my skills to aid the investigation." He held out his hand, and she gave back the map, even though she wanted to study it more.

Deputy Wadell shifted next to her and shoved his hat farther down over his forehead. He studied her as if he picked up on her tension but didn't understand the cause.

She wasn't ready to explain why Dr. Anderson's constant presence bothered her. At least now she could keep an eye on him with the search. "Is Chief McArthur planning to be part of this?"

"I don't think so." The deputy shrugged. "He asked me to stay so he can work at Eleanor's with the tech from Boston."

Mary nodded because that made perfect sense.

Henry stepped closer to her. "Is anything happening at Eleanor's?"

The young man shook his head. "Chief McArthur is setting up a tip line with help from local journalists to spread the word, but so far, nothing useful has come in." He shrugged and glanced away. "We're at a momentary standstill."

Mary smiled gently at him. "I appreciate everything you and the chief are doing."

"Mary, you're back!" Kaley hurried toward her and then reached for the bag, and Mary released it to her care. Kaley peered inside. "Is this Betty's robe?"

"Yes."

"Great! I'll see if Pipp can do anything with it." She fairly bounced with excitement.

Deputy Wadell nodded toward Dr. Anderson. "I'll help him with the grids."

"Thank you, Deputy." Mary was grateful he'd agreed to the search, even though it looked like he'd crack a tooth if he didn't find a way to release the tension tightening his jaw. And this way, he'd be with the professor while she stayed with Kaley. She turned back to her friend. "All right. Let's see what Pipp can do."

Kaley beamed as if Mary had handed her a prize. Then she knelt beside Pipp. The golden retriever looked at her with bright, intelligent eyes, his tail thumping the sidewalk in an even beat. "All right, boy. Our friend Ms. Betty needs our help. I know you can find her, because retriever is in your name. So let's go to work."

Mary opened her mouth to suggest they start somewhere Betty had been, when the dog snorted, buried his head in the bag, and yanked part of the robe out before he stuck his nose in the air. A minute later, he started pacing back and forth in a zigzag pattern across the sidewalk as if searching for something.

To Mary's surprise, Pipp seemed ready for the job. With an excited yip, he moved down the sidewalk toward the diner, dragging Kaley along with him, Mary trailing behind. Maybe he really could smell Betty's scent. Then he circled the door until Kaley was wrapped up like a Christmas package, his leash circling her legs. "Pipp!"

Mary held out a hand as Kaley delicately stepped from the constraints.

"Now, Pipp." Kaley's voice was stern as she crouched in front of her dog. The dog looked down, and his tail stopped thumping. "Ready to try again?" She set the bag in front of him, and he woofed and sniffed in circles again. Then his tail lifted high in the air, and he moved away from the Black & White Diner, gathering speed as he headed down Main Street. Mary followed, now thoroughly curious. Pipp slowed at the intersection of Main and Meeting House Road but kept moving, not caring that cars headed toward him.

Mary followed Kaley and Pipp, waving an apology to the drivers who had slammed on their brakes to avoid hitting the dog and his entourage. As she met the gaze of one of the drivers, she squinted. Could that be D.J.'s roommate? She shook her head. She hadn't spent enough time with him to recognize him in a split second of eye contact.

When Pipp reached the Grace Church parking lot, he circled, then turned around. Mary and Kaley followed, but the dog simply retraced his steps back to the diner. He circled near the front door, making it clear he had reached the same conclusion as Mary. Betty had been at the diner. It appeared Pipp had nothing new to report.

"It's okay, Pipp." Kaley got down at his level, rubbing the fur around his ears. He licked her face, then sat on his haunches and scratched an ear. "Sorry, Mary," Kaley said as they walked back to Bailey's.

"That's okay, Kaley. I so appreciate your initiative. It was a great idea."

Mary's phone rang when they reached the door to the ice-cream shop. She retrieved it from her purse, mouthed

"Excuse me" to Kaley, and stepped aside. "Hi, Eleanor. How are things going?"

"Mary, what happened? Where are you?"

"I'm at Bailey's. There's a search party here. But I'm heading to your house next."

"Good." Eleanor's voice sounded tight and strained. "Please come soon."

"Is everything okay?"

"It's fine, but I could use a familiar person."

Mary understood. "We can be there in a few minutes."

"What's up?" Henry asked as she approached him. "Should we get going?"

"I'm afraid so. Eleanor needs some moral support."

"Makes sense."

They made their way to Henry's car, and he started the engine. He eased out of the parking spot but frowned as the car lurched and made an alarming thumping sound.

"What on earth?" He stepped from the car and walked around it before opening Mary's door. "Mary, I think we need to take your car."

"Why?"

"Someone slashed my front tire."

FOURTEEN

❖

Mary's gaze met Henry's, suspicion running through her. She exited the car, then inhaled sharply when she saw the sagging tire. "Maybe we just picked up a nail...."

"Last time I had a nail, it didn't cause a gouge like that."

Mary bent and saw that the hole looked like someone had shoved in a knife and then twisted the blade. It wasn't a slash as much as it was a ragged hole. Goose bumps covered her arms.

"Oh, Henry. I'm so sorry."

"Don't worry about it. This is why I keep AAA up to date. I'll call them and catch up with you as soon as I can."

"Henry, it means so much to have you here." Mary swallowed around the lump that had settled in her throat. It seemed so unfair that his tire had been slashed when he was just trying to help her. Still, she was so grateful for his presence. "Thank you for putting everything on hold to help me."

"There's nowhere else I'd rather be, Mar."

The term of endearment pushed the lump farther into her throat as tears clogged her eyes. Henry didn't usually call her by Betty's nickname for her, but hearing it made her heart swell.

She reached for his hand, and Henry squeezed hers. "We'll find her."

Tears slipped down her cheeks, and he wiped them away. "Now go get your car and see what Eleanor needs. I promise I'll be there as soon as I can."

"Are you sure?" At his insistence, she walked the few blocks home and retrieved her car.

As she approached Eleanor's home, Mary wondered how Betty's sister-in-law had held up throughout the day. Having the police invade her elegant home couldn't be easy.

The front door opened as Mary pulled up to the curb. Eleanor stood framed in the opening, her wool pants and cashmere turtleneck topped with a matching cardigan hinting at the cold she felt. "Mary."

Mary climbed the front steps, then took Eleanor's hands. "Are you holding up?"

The elegant woman straightened her back, only the shadow in her eyes and the tremor in her fingers belying her regal posture. "The police have been a nuisance, but I'll make do. Anything to get Betty back."

Mary followed Eleanor into the large dining room where Chief McArthur leaned over the table in an intense conversation with the tech. He stood as he heard her enter.

"Chief, would you be willing to let me listen to the ransom calls?" Mary asked.

The chief looked at her with sympathy, his jowls pulled down by fatigue. "Mary, I'm not sure—"

"Please," Mary said, unwilling to give in on this. She and Chief McArthur had had their share of tense moments, but he knew he could rely on her to be discreet.

"The tech has analyzed the sounds as many ways as we can think to do it."

Mary trusted they had. Still it felt as though the day had dissipated as each of them chased wisps of trails, hunting for any hint of her sister. After she listened to the tape, she'd check on Henry, go home, and see what she could investigate on the Internet.

"Chief, Henry's tire was slashed when we stopped downtown."

"Now, Mary, don't pressure me...." The chief stopped and looked at her. "Henry's tire was slashed? Are you sure?"

"As sure as I can be. At first, I thought we'd picked up a nail, but Henry showed me the gouge in the tire. It had to be intentional."

Chief McArthur frowned. "I don't like this at all, Mary. There's only one person I can think of who would want to slow you down."

Mary met his gaze. "The kidnapper?"

"It makes sense. Do you know where Henry is having the car towed?"

"No, but I can call him and find out." Mary pulled out her phone and noticed the time. It was almost 7:00 PM, creeping up on the twenty-four-hour mark. A milestone she still hoped to avoid.

Someone knocked on the door, and Eleanor excused herself, only to return a moment later with Henry and Evan.

"AAA arrived quickly." Henry gestured toward Evan. "Evan offered to give me a ride."

Mary's nephew shrugged, and his face wore a woebegone expression. "Nobody really needed me downtown. Deputy

Wadell and Dr. Anderson were busy getting people organized, and I was just in the way."

The chief looked at Henry. "Mary was just telling me about your trouble. You're sure it was slashed?"

"Sure as I can be. We weren't having any trouble before we stopped, and after we got back in the car, it was flat with a big gouge cut into it."

Chief McArthur grimaced. "I don't like this one bit. Where did you have the car towed? I'd like to get a tech down there, just in case we can find anything on the tire."

"Sure. The tow truck's hauling it to Bob's Repair Shop. Would you like me to get you the number?"

"Just ask them to leave it alone until I get someone there."

Henry looked at him quizzically. "Do you really think they can find something?"

"Not sure, but it's worth trying."

"All right." Henry stepped away, digging his phone from his pocket as he left.

The thought that the kidnapper had followed them and slashed their tire left Mary cold. Was Betty still safe? "Have we received proof of life yet?" Chief McArthur shook his head, and her stomach tensed. "Should I worry?"

Chief McArthur shrugged. "It's hard to say. Maybe he's keeping her somewhere different than where he was when he first called." The chief settled on the edge of a chair, looking ready to spring into action any moment. "If he has her tucked somewhere out of the way, then he has logistical issues to work through. The good news is this buys us more time to find her."

"As long as he doesn't grow tired and walk away. Could this be spontaneous? I mean, he had to know something, but it seems the details are loose."

As Henry returned and stepped close to Mary, she welcomed his calming presence. He had been her rock throughout the day. What would she have done without him?

"I just talked to Bob, and he said he'd keep everyone away from my car until you get someone down there."

"Thanks, Henry," the chief said. "I'll send someone to check the tire. Now, Mary, don't get your hopes up. I don't think it's likely we'll get anything, but maybe we'll find fingerprints or other trace evidence." He looked at her. "Please promise you won't get your hopes up."

"I'll try." But because she so badly wanted Betty home before another night passed, it would be hard not to hope some evidence waited on the tire.

The chief ran a hand over his head, then nodded. "Let's have you listen to the call while I get someone to check on the tire." Chief McArthur gestured toward the electronic equipment set up on Eleanor's walnut table. Mary could barely see the burgundy tablecloth beneath the paraphernalia scattered across its surface. "This is Stephanie Wetli with the Boston PD. She's on loan for at least another day, until we have the delivery instructions."

Mary shook hands with the petite woman with a smattering of freckles across her peaches-and-cream complexion, a soft smile, and a hint of wisdom in her eyes.

"Wish we were meeting under different circumstances." South Boston accented Officer Wetli's words.

"Thank you."

"Let her listen to the call as many times as she'd like," Chief McArthur said. "I'll be back after I make this call."

"All right." Officer Wetli picked up a pair of earphones. "Slip these on, and I'll replay it for you as many times as you need."

Mary slipped the headset in place and concentrated. Silence turned into a moment of static before a man's voice started. The voice was gruff, sounding like he'd swallowed mouthfuls of gravel. It was hard to gauge age or anything distinctive from the muffled and disguised voice. His word choice was clean and seemed educated.

"Mrs. Blakely, I'll tell you again. You have twenty-four hours to collect fifty thousand dollars. Small bills. Nothing larger than a twenty-dollar bill. I will call back in the morning with instructions on delivery."

Eleanor broke in, sounding regal and composed. *"I demand proof of life."*

"I won't be ordered around."

"Neither will I. Prove my sister-in-law is alive, or I won't comply."

A muffled curse was almost filtered out. *"Watch your front porch."* Then the call ended.

Mary frowned. That was it? "Can you play it again?"

Officer Wetli complied. Mary jotted notes on a piece of paper she'd pulled from her purse as she listened a second time.

"How can there be no background noise? It's like he called from a bubble."

"I've run it through several filters but haven't found anything discernible." Officer Wetli gestured to the headset. "Would you like to listen again?"

"Yes, then can Henry?"

Officer Wetli glanced at Chief McArthur, who nodded even though he still had his phone glued to his ear.

As Mary listened, she checked what she'd written down, then gave the headphones to Henry. "And you weren't able to trace the call?"

Officer Wetli shook her head. "Despite what TV shows demonstrate, it takes a bit of time to actually run the trace. I could narrow it down to a thirty-mile radius around Ivy Bay."

"Not very helpful, is it?"

"No." The officer started the playback for Henry once he had the headphones in place. "He must watch a lot of TV, because he ended the call too quickly."

"Of course." Mary sighed as she sank onto a dining room chair. "I just hoped you would have learned more from the call." She looked at her nephew, who sat at the table, intently staring at the hands he'd clasped in front of him. "Evan, do you want to listen?"

"If you didn't hear anything, Aunt Mary, I doubt I will." Still he shifted to accept the headphones when Henry finished and listened once.

Mary wondered where Betty could be. Thirty miles was a broad circle around Ivy Bay. For all Mary knew, her sister could be on a boat in the middle of the bay.

A phone rang, and Evan jerked off the headset as everyone froze.

Eleanor looked at Officer Wetli, who held up a finger as she flipped a couple of switches, handed the headset to Chief McArthur, then nodded.

Eleanor picked up the phone from the table. "This is Eleanor."

She nodded, then opened her mouth. "Are you sure..." She clamped her mouth shut and slammed the phone down. "He hung up."

Officer Wetli played with her equipment while Chief McArthur pulled out his notebook. "I couldn't hear anything through the headphones. Tell me every word he said."

"That's simple. It was a short message, though his voice was garbled this time. 'Check your e-mail.'"

"Your e-mail? What about the porch?" McArthur was headed toward the door before Eleanor confirmed. "But you've never given him your e-mail address."

"I know." Eleanor wrung her hands. "But that's all he said. He must have e-mailed me something."

Mary's hands turned clammy, and her head felt faint as she watched Eleanor flip open her laptop. With a few keystrokes, her e-mail opened as Chief McArthur walked back from the front door, his hands conspicuously empty. A prayer churned through Mary's thoughts, over and over. *Please keep her safe, please keep her safe, please keep Betty safe.*

An e-mail popped up at the top of the in-box, with the subject line: Proof of life. So much communicated in those few simple words. Mary fought to gather a breath, as Henry took her hand and squeezed it.

Eleanor pivoted to look at Chief McArthur. "Should I open it?" At his nod, she clicked on the icon, then on the attachment.

A second later, Betty's face stared at them from the screen. She looked directly at the camera, weariness coating her face, pulling down her cheeks, dark circles under her eyes. Her hair was limp around her cheeks. Other than that, she looked just as she had the morning before at breakfast.

"Mom's all right." Evan breathed out the words, a husky tone in his voice, then repeated them in a shout. "Mom's okay." He slapped the chief on the back, letting out a whoop.

Eleanor scrolled down, revealing a newspaper in Betty's hands, but the background showed little—only a beige wall, with nothing distinguishable on it.

As Mary watched, she noticed a time stamp. "This photo was taken at five, only two hours ago." Some of the tension leeched from her muscles. "Thank You, Jesus."

A chorus of amens joined her.

Mary continued to study the picture. "Why the delay e-mailing it?"

Chief McArthur leaned in on the other side of Eleanor. "The paper is today's *Boston Globe*." He slammed a hand on the table. "The kidnapper could have picked that up anywhere. Why couldn't he pick a local paper that helps us narrow down where he's keeping Betty?"

Officer Wetli pointed at a corner of the photo. "It looks like something is here. I'll try to clean the file and see if I can identify that and anything else that isn't immediately clear."

"Can you trace the photo?" Mary knew it was a long shot but had to check.

"I'll check for that too." Officer Wetli clicked around on her computer, pulling up different programs. "It all depends on how savvy the kidnapper is. Some send photos loaded with data they don't realize is embedded in the file. Others send a photo with nothing useful." She pointed to the paper. "My guess is he will turn out to be savvy. He could have grabbed your local paper or that of another small town, but instead, he chose the one that's available across Massachusetts and the region."

Chief McArthur pushed away from the table and paced across the room. "He's going to make a mistake. Sooner or later, they all do." He stopped and his gaze met Mary's. "We will be ready when he does. I promise you."

"Thank you, Chief. I know you are doing your best." Mary could only pray this kidnapper's mistake would come soon, before something happened to her sister. Her gaze traveled back to Betty on the computer screen. She was alive, and the kidnapper hadn't made any threats that suggested that would change. Mary would cling to that knowledge while she prayed for help and searched for a break in the case.

"Eleanor, will you forward that e-mail to me?"

"Absolutely." With a few clicks, Eleanor had the message zinging through cyberspace. While the tech completed her checks of the photo, Mary would do the same.

Maybe, just maybe, with all of them working together, they'd find something that led to the kidnapper.

FIFTEEN

·◆◆·

In the silence that followed, Mary looked to Henry. He sent a small smile her way, then pointed toward the front door.

"How about I get everyone subs from Pizzeria Rustica?"

Mary's stomach rumbled, reminding her she hadn't eaten anything since the sandwich Henry had made hours earlier. Even the granola bars she'd grabbed still sat in her purse, completely unappetizing in the light of Henry's offer. "Sounds like a great idea."

Henry collected everyone's orders, then came alongside Mary. "Can I take your car?" She handed him her keys, then smiled as he saluted her. "Don't go anywhere without me."

"How can I?" she said, laughing. "You'll have the car."

Once Henry left, Mary wasn't sure what to do to be helpful except stay out of the chief's and technician's way. The officer pecked away at her keyboard with an intensity that didn't stray. Still, as Mary watched, it seemed all the officer's efforts failed to produce anything. Eleanor had disappeared into her kitchen, while Evan sat on the sofa, a blank look on his face as he texted someone.

Mary pulled her small notebook from her purse and opened it. She reviewed the few notes about what she'd learned from D.J., then turned to a new page.

"I might have something," Officer Wetli said before Mary could write anything down. The technician pointed at her screen.

When Mary reached her, she saw that the screen showed different locations popping up. "What is this?"

"It's my attempt to backtrack to the sender's location."

"How do you do that?"

"By tracing the IP address. All computers and servers have them. Each is unique and serves as a locator." Locations continued to pop up, and the technician slumped in her chair. "Unfortunately, whoever sent this knew what he was doing. This is pinging all over the world."

"So we can't locate where it originated?"

"Not likely with the tools I have here. I'll forward it to another technician. He may have better luck." With a few keystrokes, she opened another window and soon had an e-mail sent.

Mary sank onto a chair at the table with a groan. She'd known better than to assume the photo would lead them directly to Betty. However, she'd still hoped the technician's efforts to locate the information from the photo would at least narrow down the scope of the search so Betty wouldn't spend another night alone and dependent on a kidnapper.

"So we don't have any sense of where he took Betty," she said.

Chief McArthur stepped around the table. "We'll keep looking, Mary. You heard Officer Wetli. That photo will be scoured, and there are more resources in Boston. There's still a chance we can unwind the data about where it was taken."

Mary sighed as she shifted in her chair. "We're assuming he didn't scrub it clean. If he shifted the IP address all over the world, he probably removed all the data too."

"Maybe, but remember, everybody makes mistakes, Mary, and we'll find his. The key is persistent digging. I promise we'll find him."

She believed him. Chief McArthur was very good at what he did, and she'd watched him in enough situations to know he never let an investigation end until he'd wrestled it to a conclusion.

The front door opened, and a moment later, Henry walked into the room with two bags of sandwiches. As he distributed sandwiches and Eleanor brought drinks from the kitchen, Mary returned to the couch, waiting to receive her dinner.

Henry sat in the chair next to the couch but didn't give her a sandwich. "Are you busy?"

"Not at the moment." Unfortunately, she had nothing to do here but felt compelled to stay since she'd run out of ideas. She hadn't added a thing to her notes, either, while Henry had run for food. Maybe it was time to head home now that Henry was back with her car. At home, she could dig into some investigating using her laptop.

"Good."

"Good?"

"I'm taking you home and giving you a chance to relax and eat your sandwich in peace. Maybe there you'll make the connections you're so good at seeing."

"What if I miss something here?"

Her gaze followed his as he turned to Eleanor. The poor woman yawned as she lifted her sandwich to take a bite. She set her sandwich down on its china plate and dabbed her mouth with a linen napkin.

"Eleanor, you'll be here all night, right?" Henry asked.

"Of course." Eleanor yawned again. "At most, I'll curl up on the couch and wait for another call."

Next he turned to the police chief. "Chief McArthur, you'll call Mary the moment you need anything or have something to report, right?"

"Absolutely." The chief looked at his watch. "I'll step away only long enough to compare notes with Deputy Wadell, but Officer Wetli knows how to reach me."

Henry turned back to Mary, but she stopped him with a raised hand and a smile. "Point taken, Henry Woodrow. Going home sounds nice."

When they arrived at her home, Mary felt a heaviness settle on her again. Coming home wouldn't be the same until Betty returned, but Henry was right. She was more likely to see things differently if she wasn't on edge at Eleanor's, praying for the phone to ring.

As they walked inside, Gus hurried down the stairs with a loud meow. The gray cat stopped at Mary's feet and looked up at her.

"We're still looking, buddy."

"Your momma's working hard."

Gus meowed as if to say of course she was. Then he led the way to the kitchen.

Mary walked to the refrigerator and pulled out some iced tea, while Henry set the bag of sandwiches and chips on the table.

"I'll bring the food to you, Mary. Prop your feet up and rest. It's okay to *just be* for a bit."

Mary nodded, knowing an argument with him wouldn't get her anywhere. He was determined to serve her in this way, and she needed to let him.

Still bundled in her coat because she couldn't shake a chill, Mary wandered into the sunroom. Often she sensed God's presence and His still voice best from the upholstered reading bench, so many mornings, she sat out here and watched the sun rise over the ocean, marveling at God's creative genius, each sunrise different yet the same. If she opened the windows, she'd hear the steady pulse of the ocean's waves knocking against the shore in an unending battle.

While she waited, she didn't sense God's voice, but peace settled over her. It was almost as if He whispered to her heart that all would be well, He had Betty in His hands, and she didn't need to fear.

Mary inhaled, then blew out slowly. She breathed in the peace, grateful for the gift it was.

Henry stepped around the corner. "Ready to eat?"

"Absolutely."

When she sat down at the kitchen table, a plate filled with a sub—just the way she liked it—and a serving of sliced fruit waited. A bag of kettle chips sat next to a glass of tea.

"This looks great, Henry. Thank you."

"It's my pleasure." He sat down and settled a napkin across his lap.

She reached for his hand and waited until he met her gaze. "I mean it. Everything you've done for me today."

"I'm always here for you, Mary. Anything you need, just ask."

"Thank you." Mary waited for him to pray, then picked up her fork and took a bite of fruit. Silence settled as they both focused on eating. When they were done and had cleaned up the kitchen, Mary walked Henry to the door. "Can I give you a ride home?"

"No, it's a long walk, but it'll help me unwind. Are you sure you don't want me to stay?"

"Absolutely." Mary handed him his coat. "You've already done so much, and I know you have other things to do."

He studied her intently. "Okay, I'll leave, but only if you promise to call if anything happens or you need me."

"I promise."

"Any time of the night."

"Yes, sir." She saluted with a grin, then opened the door. "I'll be fine, Henry."

"I know." He gave her a hug, then walked onto the front porch. "See you in the morning."

She watched as he walked down the sidewalk and disappeared into the night. Then she slowly closed the door. The house felt empty, as if half its heart had stopped beating. At least last night's phone call and this evening's photo affirmed Betty was safe. So far, the kidnapper had done nothing to harm her sister. Mary wandered into the living room and settled onto the blue-and-white-striped couch with a notebook and pen.

She wasn't exactly sure where to start, so she reviewed the list of the people she'd talked to during the day. The list wasn't long: Pastor Miles and Margie at Grace Church, Kaley Court at the grocery store, Nicole Hancock at the Black & White Diner, Charlene Bellingham at the garden center, Marnie and a host of people such as Susan and Sophie who were concerned but didn't know a thing about Betty's disappearance. Mary added Henry, Evan, and Eleanor. Then she started a separate list with the police: Chief McArthur, Deputy Wadell, Officer Wetli, and Don Laux. There was one more person, but she hesitated. Where did Dr. Jonathan Anderson fit? She debated it for a moment, then finally listed him to the side near Nicole and Charlene.

She glanced over her lists and realized she'd skipped D.J. Because he'd been the last person to see Betty outside the diner, she added him, just to be thorough. Then the thought hit her: tuition and fees at an institution such as MIT were expensive. Could they be so expensive they'd cause him to kidnap Betty? D.J. also mentioned needing an investor for his business idea, an idea he seemed very passionate about and determined to make succeed.

Mary shook her head. There was no way D.J.'s money needs could be dire enough to lead him to kidnap his mother's cousin. It made no sense.

She looked at her short lists. Deputy Bobby Wadell's name was the next to jump out at her.

The deputy clearly had money concerns, as the call she'd overheard highlighted, but that did not mean he was involved. She resisted believing he could be, especially when she'd worked with him on different mysteries. He'd always been courteous and conscientious. But she couldn't deny that the deputy had been intense to the point of brooding, which was out of character. Was it a coincidence?

And why had Deputy Wadell been so intent on discouraging a search when he seemed to know how to organize one? Why the combativeness? Did he have a reason for not wanting Betty found?

Mary shook off the thought. It seemed implausible, until she considered his clear money woes. Could those be enough to give him a reason to try kidnapping to raise funds? She didn't want to think so but made a note to investigate anyway.

Mary tossed the notebook aside. She needed to do something. She grabbed her laptop from her room and returned to the living room couch. Gus settled next to her, front paws planted on her thigh, his body turned so he faced her. He reached up and tapped her cheek with a paw, as if asking if she was okay. She stroked his fur, and after a minute, he settled down and purred as she continued.

Where to start? It shouldn't take long to see just how expensive D.J.'s MIT tuition was, which would help her grasp his money needs. With a few clicks, Mary opened a search engine and then found the MIT page that delineated the expenses an undergrad could expect to pay. Tuition alone was fifty-seven thousand dollars. Then add fees, an apartment, minimal expenses for food and surviving, and the price tag grew steeper.

She rubbed Gus's silky ears. "Guess I should be glad my kids went to college twenty years ago."

Gus looked up and meowed. Then he plopped his head on his front paws, keeping his eyes open to watch her.

With prices like that, Mary could understand why Jean had complained about the expense and wondered how her son would pay. It also provided a strong reason for D.J. to focus on launching his business idea. With those costs, he'd have plenty of bills when he graduated.

But that didn't make him a kidnapper.

SIXTEEN

——◆◆——

Mary closed her eyes and took several deep breaths. She felt antsy, yet listless. Worried and unfocused. What she needed was prayer.

Dear Lord, I need Your guidance, Your peace. I am at a loss, and, Lord, so desperate to find my sister. Please lead me, the police, or the searchers to Betty. Please keep her safe, and surround her with Your love. I pray for Your wisdom and insight.

She opened her eyes and was about to grab her Bible off the side table when a thought struck her. Dr. Anderson was a frequent visitor to Ivy Bay, and he had a small cabin just outside of town. He'd shown up everywhere today, yet she knew almost nothing about him. Maybe with a little research, she'd develop a better understanding of why he'd appeared.

After entering search terms, she started clicking through a series of articles. The first talked about Dr. Anderson's consulting work with the police department in Rhode Island. Another pointed to a competitive grant he'd applied for so his research in the interrelationships between biology and technology could continue. She checked the date and noted it was from late November. The following article interviewed him after learning he hadn't won the grant.

She noticed a video on the sidebar and clicked the link. A minute later, she was watching Dr. Anderson explain his disappointment and commitment. "I am absolutely committed to this research. I've seen data that tells me I'm on the trail of the key to understanding foundational principles." He looked away from the camera and swallowed hard. "I will do all I can to find the needed funding." He turned and walked away from the camera and the reporter's continuing questions.

After the video ended, Mary sat, the rumble of Gus's purr the only sound. "What could he be researching, Gus?"

The cat looked up at the mention of his name, then started cleaning a paw.

Mary backtracked to the links she'd found, but after clicking through to several, she was no closer to understanding his research. The articles she found were too scientific for her to wade through. Would the lack of research funding make the professor desperate enough to kidnap someone? It could possibly explain a motive.

Was there another approach she should take? A couple of people had mentioned Dr. Anderson's cabin outside of town. A cabin would be the perfect place to keep Betty while waiting for the ransom. She needed to learn where the professor's cabin was located. Mary grabbed the phone book from the kitchen but didn't find Dr. Anderson, so she entered his name in a property search. A minute later, she had his address and noted it. She looked at her watch, itching to go do something. Drive to the cabin. See if anyone was there.

Something restrained her.

Maybe it was her promise to Henry. Maybe it was the realization that this was something she should really let the police do. She grabbed her cell phone and dialed the chief.

It took a while, but he answered the call.

"Hi, Mary. What's up?"

"Hi, Chief. Sorry for calling this late, but I had an odd thought."

"You caught me at the station. So what can I do for you?"

She took a breath, wondering if he would consider her latest thought. "Today, I kept bumping into someone. In fact, I may be paranoid, but he seemed to be following me. His name is Jonathan Anderson."

"I know Dr. Anderson. What about him?"

Mary felt a little silly. If the chief knew Dr. Anderson, and wasn't suspicious, should she be? "Well, do you think he could be involved? I know it's a stretch, but he was almost everywhere I went today."

"Jonathan?" The chief coughed as if something had gone down the wrong pipe. "I hadn't considered it. He's always seemed the picture of the absentminded professor."

"Here's the thing. I know it's a reach, but what else do we have right now? I did some research, and he may have motive. I discovered he has a research project he's passionate about, but it was denied funding. And he has a cabin on the outskirts of town. An isolated cabin seems an awfully convenient place for a kidnapper to operate. Shouldn't we check if Betty is there?"

The chief didn't respond immediately, as if he was considering her proposal. "I think this is a reach, Mary, but I trust your instincts. If you think we should check it out, I'll drive by on my way home in a few minutes, but I wouldn't expect much."

"I won't, Chief. I honestly don't know what to think about him. But if you'd check, I'd sleep better tonight."

"If it'll put your mind at ease, I'm glad to do it. I'll call you after I see Jonathan. Try to get some rest, Mary."

"Thank you." Mary hung up. Rest should be what her body craved, but nervous energy surged through her, so she wandered to the kitchen and heated the quiche Sophie had given her. As she ate, she wondered if it was possible Dr. Anderson knew Eleanor. If so, that would be more understandable than Mary's earlier idea that D.J. was the professor's connection to Betty. After Mary put her plate in the sink, she dialed Eleanor, who picked up after a couple of rings.

"Don't you ever sleep, Mary?" Eleanor sounded exhausted, as if Mary's call had woken her.

"Hello, Eleanor." Mary glanced at the clock and groaned. "I'm so sorry to call this late. I guess I got swept up in my thoughts. I'll keep this quick. Do you know Jonathan Anderson?"

"Who?"

"Dr. Jonathan Anderson. He's a professor at MIT."

Eleanor was silent, and Mary let it stretch, giving the other woman time to think. "Actually, yes. He came by the house a couple of times this winter."

Mary grabbed her notebook and made a note. "Oh? When?"

"I don't remember the exact dates."

"But he's been inside your house?"

One moment in Eleanor's home and the professor would have a sense of her personal wealth from the tasteful way the house was decorated with antiques and rich rugs. Each item pointed to a person who had enough money to have only the best in her home.

"Yes, of course," Eleanor said. "Does it matter?"

"I'm not sure." Mary paused, trying to think of a way to explain her concerns without sounding like her thoughts had roamed too far in her efforts to find Betty. "He's appeared almost everywhere I went today. What can you tell me about him?"

"He's a nice man. Smart, well spoken, and exactly what you'd expect of a professor at a school like MIT." Eleanor chuckled, then continued. "Sometimes he's a bit dull, but he can be an entertaining addition to a dinner party when he's in town and inclined to join."

"Why did he come this winter?"

"There's some project he's working on currently. Somehow it's related to what my husband did, and so Dr. Anderson has come a few times to read through his papers."

Mary thought about that a moment. "So he came to review files?"

"The strange thing was that after he'd read them, he asked for money. He claimed he didn't have enough to continue his research, so I should help since his area was so closely tied to my husband's."

"Did you?"

"No. I didn't have the slightest interest."

Could this be the same research the articles and video had mentioned? If it was, it gave Dr. Anderson a funding need, knowledge that Eleanor had resources, and a reason to target her with the ransom demand. "How much did he request?"

"Sixty thousand dollars. He must think I'm made of money and should donate large sums to him."

"How did he take your decision?"

"He was disappointed." Eleanor hesitated, then continued: "In fact, he returned at least once, asking me to reconsider. He didn't appreciate how firm I was on the matter."

Mary smiled because she'd learned Eleanor could be quite firm in her decisions. At times like this, when it came to paying the ransom demand, Mary was grateful.

"He refused to believe I'd rather not give any of my money to higher education. Normally, I'd be quite open to funding education but not for a project I don't understand."

Mary could appreciate Eleanor's reasoning. "Thanks, Eleanor."

After they hung up, Mary turned back to her list. Jonathan Anderson was at the very top of her suspect list. For now, she'd wait to hear what the chief had to say about the doctor's cabin.

Gus pranced into the kitchen, his back arched and fur standing on end.

"Gus?" Mary reached down to pick him up, but he skittered back and hissed. "What's wrong, boy?"

He backed down the hall, ears pricking in a nonstop swivel as if he heard something but wasn't sure what it was. What had gotten into her normally placid cat?

"Are you all right?" She followed him into the hall but froze when she heard a screech.

What had made that sound?

She took a step forward into the silence, then heard another sound as if someone had stepped on one of the porch boards that needed to be tightened.

Was someone standing on the porch?

Mary waited a minute to see if whoever it was would ring the doorbell. Only silence settled as she paused. Maybe she'd allowed her mind to get carried away with everything that had happened.

After another minute, she looked at Gus, who stood facing the door, focused intently on something. "This is ridiculous, Gus."

She marched to the door and looked through the peephole. The limited view of the porch and front yard revealed nothing out of the ordinary. With a puff of released breath, Mary unlocked the door and pulled it open. Gus rushed past her, brushing her pant leg. She squinted to see in the darkness but couldn't make out anything.

Gus meowed, and she glanced at him. He pawed at a bauble that glinted in the light spilling from behind Mary.

"What do you have?" Mary squatted next to Gus, who batted the piece of silver. Mary picked it up and stiffened.

It was one of Betty's silver Tiffany earrings.

How had it gotten there? In Mary's experience, earrings fell out a little too often. But that was usually because Mary was a bit lazy with them, often forgetting to take them out when she slept. She remembered one instance in which she'd lost a small diamond earring John had bought her, and to this day, she felt a surge of guilt when she was reminded of it.

But Betty was different. She was organized and meticulous about her bedtime routine and bought only the highest quality jewelry with secure backings.

Of course, accidents happened. But this was the first new sign of Betty that Mary had seen since yesterday, and her heart raced at the thought that it could be a clue. Plus, she hadn't seen it when she'd been on the porch earlier that day.

If the earring *hadn't* been there earlier, did that mean someone had left it for Mary to find? If so, why? There was no guarantee she would have noticed such a small bauble.

She flipped on the porch light, then crouched to her hands and knees and scanned the porch. A scrap of paper flapped under the edge of the welcome mat. Mary grabbed it, and after one more glance around the yard, stepped inside to read the note.

Back off, or your sister loses more than an earring.

SEVENTEEN

Mary's hands trembled as she read the stark, threatening words scrawled in block letters. She set the piece of paper on the hall table and instinctively backed away.

The words were a clear threat. Something much worse could happen to Betty if Mary kept searching, but how could she stop?

Mary dragged in a ragged breath that didn't seem to fill her lungs. She sucked deeper, tugging in a lungful of air, then raced down the hall to the kitchen. Chief McArthur would want to know about the note and earring. He didn't answer, so she left a voice mail.

She circled the first floor of the house, looking out the windows, but it was hard to see into the darkness. The kidnapper had left the note and earring on her porch, and now she couldn't shake the heebie-jeebies, feeling as if someone were watching her. She doubted that was the case, but still, she circled the rooms again, this time tightly closing the curtains before moving back into the kitchen and turning on a stove burner. Maybe a mug of lavender chamomile tea would calm her and focus her thoughts.

She filled the teakettle and set it on a back burner. As it heated, she pulled out a mug and tea bag, unable to shake the unease that had settled between her shoulder blades. She fidgeted in place, willing the water to boil and the chief to call her back.

She leaned against the counter and felt her cell phone press into her hip. She reached into her pocket and pulled it out.

At the garden center, she'd taken a photo of the receipt the police had found in Betty's car. She hadn't thought about it since, but she could look at it while she waited and see if there was anything that scrap of paper could tell her that would help with the search. She doubted it, but at this point, she was grasping at straws.

The phone rang in her hand. "Hello."

"Mary." The chief sounded tired, as if he still hadn't made it home. "You called?"

"Chief, could you come by? The kidnapper left one of Betty's earrings and a note on my front porch." A fresh shiver shook her at the thought of how close the kidnapper had been.

"I'll be right there."

"Thank you."

When she hung up, Mary noticed the burble of the teakettle. She poured hot water over the tea bag.

As the tea steeped, she clicked a few buttons on her phone and pulled up the image of Betty's receipt. It was for a meal at Sam's Seafood from Monday, the day before Betty was kidnapped. Located in an old, low cottage by the marina, Sam's was a dive Betty enjoyed, so Mary wasn't surprised to see she'd eaten there. It wasn't unusual for them to meet and enjoy a meal of fish and chips with friends.

As she examined the receipt, Mary saw that it was for one lunch meal. Mary tried to remember what Betty had planned for Monday. It would be unusual but not improbable for her to eat out alone, especially if she wanted to grab a quick bite between engagements.

Mary looked at what Betty had ordered and stopped.

Crab, with a note for it to be extra spicy? Betty would never order a dish like that.

Mary heard steps on the porch and then a knock. She hurried down the hall to peek through the peephole. It was the chief. The dark circles under his eyes emphasized that it had been a long twenty-four hours since Betty had called with her startling message.

She opened the door, and he nodded. "Mary, I got here as quickly as I could. Would you like me to check the outside of the house?"

She hadn't planned to ask, but the thought of knowing no one lingered comforted her. "Thank you."

"It'll just take a moment." A few minutes later, he returned. "I didn't see anyone. Do you have the message? And did you say an earring?"

"Yes. I have them right here." Mary gestured to the hall table. "I touched the earring and note without thinking. I'm sorry."

"It's understandable." He stepped past her, slipped on gloves, and picked up the items. "*Hmm.* Short and to the point."

"That's what I thought too."

He slipped the note and earring in a paper bag he'd brought with him. "Between this and Henry's tire, I think you've got the kidnapper's attention. Any idea why?"

"Not really. I only talked to a few people." Mary gave him the brief summary. "That's all." She slumped from the fatigue and questions racing through her mind. "Am I closer than I think?" And if she was, why couldn't she see why the kidnapper was concerned?

"I don't know, but I wish I did. Then we'd be closer to finding this guy. Please be careful, Mary. Whoever is behind this doesn't appreciate you poking around." He took off his cap and rubbed his head before settling the cap back in place. "Do you have any idea why he's focused on you?"

She thought about her day again, but still nothing jumped out at her. "There has to be something, but I can't imagine what. Since I found Betty's car at the garden center, it feels like I've wandered in circles."

"I know that feeling." His smile was rueful. "The kidnapper probably assumes it's easier to intimidate a lone woman than the entire Ivy Bay Police Department." He looked at her with warm affection. "Poor sap."

His words made Mary feel a little better. But only a little. "What should I do now, Chief? Sit on my hands and wait here?" She grimaced at the thought.

"I don't know, Mary, but that might be best for Betty and you."

She opened her mouth to protest, but something stopped her. Could she inadvertently have done something that made the kidnapper feel cornered or angry without understanding how close she'd come to him? Maybe she could uncover what that was if she thought long enough. Then she considered her lists and the circles they took her through. "I just want Betty home. Do you know how the search went today? The one Deputy Wadell helped organize for the town?"

"They didn't find anything. Though I don't think either of us expected them to." Mary shook her head sadly, and the chief patted her on the shoulder. "We're working night and day on this, Mary. Promise me you'll be very careful tomorrow. The initial report back on Henry's tire is that there are no discernible fingerprints. It was a long shot, but we do know someone was mad enough to slash a tire while the car was downtown. In daylight."

"I promise I'll be careful."

He studied her closely, as if trying to see to her deepest intentions. "One call from the kidnapper tomorrow and we'll have the ransom ready to deliver. Remember that. And I'm serious, Mary. Whoever this is, he isn't acting rationally."

"I understand." And she did. She needed to be careful moving forward not to make the kidnapper feel threatened. He knew her, who she was, where she lived. Another thought occurred to her. "Did you get a chance to go by Jonathan Anderson's cottage?"

The chief sighed. "I did. He wasn't home."

"Did you look around?" Mary persisted. "Did you look for anything suspicious?"

"I can't do that without a warrant, Mary. You know that." He sighed again. Mary wondered if he'd slept since the ransom call the night before. "Call me if you need anything tonight."

"I will. Thank you for coming out again."

Mary watched the chief walk out to his cruiser. As soon as she closed and bolted the front door, Mary set the house alarm, then returned to the kitchen and picked up her cell phone.

In a moment, she had reopened the receipt. Why would Betty have requested extra-spicy food? Mary couldn't imagine she had.

Which meant it couldn't be Betty's receipt. Could the kidnapper have dropped this receipt in Betty's car?

Mary's heart leaped at the thought. If the receipt was the kidnapper's, that meant he had been in Ivy Bay the day before the kidnapping, which was new information. It could mean he lived in Ivy Bay, something Mary didn't doubt, given that he seemed to know Eleanor and Betty enough to understand their relationship and the fact that Eleanor had money. He also knew where Mary lived.

Of course, he could also be a part-time resident of Ivy Bay. Dr. Anderson's face flashed in Mary's mind.

She needed to figure out who paid for this meal. Taking the receipt to Sam's might lead to a credit-card payment. That would lead to a name, which the police could track to the person.

She took a deep breath. The receipt might not lead anywhere. But first thing in the morning after the restaurant opened, Mary would be there.

Mary took a sip of her lukewarm tea, then returned to the couch and her laptop. The clock might tell her it was almost 11:00 PM, but her nerves were too jumpy to pretend to go to sleep.

She tried to do a quick search of the bankruptcy records and see if Dr. Anderson or Deputy Wadell had ever filed, but it quickly became apparent that she couldn't search bankruptcy records without a specialized account.

She thought for a few moments, then entered Deputy Wadell's name into the search engine and stilled as she scrolled through the results. On the second page of search results was a link to an article about a kidnapping that had occurred a few years earlier in western Massachusetts. Deputy Wadell had been a young officer on the small-town force who had participated in the search. The results had been disastrous, as the search had cornered the kidnapper.

After reading a couple more articles on that kidnapping, Mary's initial take was affirmed. Deputy Wadell had seen a kidnapping go horribly wrong. In the earlier case, police believed the kidnapping victim would have survived if a spontaneous search hadn't organically appeared out of nowhere, spooking the kidnappers. Without knowing it, the volunteers had approached the house where the victim was held. The next day, when police arrived, the kidnapping victim was dead. This could explain the deputy's strong hot and cold reactions to the attempts to search for Betty.

The one search he'd been involved in had ended poorly. He knew the basics of how to organize one, but the end result in that prior case had been tragic. Did Deputy Wadell fear the same could happen to Betty? He might be right, but that didn't mean they shouldn't try.

Betty was counting on the fact that Mary would be looking for her; in fact, she had signaled she knew it by adding "hang ten" to her message. If only Mary knew what her sister meant by using that phrase.

Mary shut her laptop and prayed that despite what she'd read and the earring left on her front porch that Betty was sleeping well. Maybe in time, Mary could do the same.

EIGHTEEN

Morning light streamed through Mary's windows, teasing her awake from the shadowy images of Deputy Wadell's earlier kidnapping case that filled her dreams. Gus had curled on top of the comforter at her feet, as if he'd sensed her distress. Even with his comforting presence, she sensed the emptiness that filled the house without Betty, the fears left by the kidnapper along with Betty's earring and the note. It was more than knowing Betty wasn't down the stairs and around the corner that left Mary feeling her sister's absence. She looked at the clock. Already eight o'clock?

While struggling to fall asleep last night, Mary had decided to drive by Professor Anderson's cabin herself this morning. She also planned to stop at Sam's Seafood.

After a quick shower, Mary got dressed and then carried her Bible downstairs. She fixed a bowl of cereal and a mug of coffee, doctored just the way she liked it. After a quick prayer, she ate her breakfast and planned her day.

Sam's didn't open for a couple of hours. Hopefully the waitstaff would remember who had ordered spicy crab earlier that week. Then she would drive by Professor Anderson's cottage and confirm whether D.J. had ever talked to him about his family. She knew those were two good, strong leads on Betty's kidnapper, but it still didn't feel like enough. If she only knew what she'd discovered yesterday that had caused the kidnapper to threaten her.

Mary opened her Bible to the Psalms, and her gaze fell on Psalm 68. Her pulse slowed as she read David's promise that God was "a father to the fatherless, a defender of widows." That was what she needed—to accept and believe God was Betty's defender. That when she couldn't be there to help Betty, God was already there. He was faithful and His promises never changed. What was true for David was also true today.

Mary read the verses again. God was a defender of widows.

Thankfulness rose up in her heart, and she turned the words into a prayer that God would be with Betty, that He would surround her and shield her throughout whatever the day brought, and that she would know she was not alone.

Mary needed that promise as well. *God, show me what to do and where to go.*

She pushed away from the table. The house felt too quiet, so she turned on the TV, then retrieved her phone and settled on the couch. With the news playing in the background, she pulled up her copy of the kidnapper's proof-of-life photo. She wished Betty were home so Mary could wipe the lines from her sister's face.

A story on the news captured her attention because it involved a cell phone superimposed on the corner of a photo. Mary turned up the volume and listened as the reporter talked about the different information embedded in photos taken by cell phones and some cameras. The reporter indicated it would take a fairly sophisticated person to scrub the information from photos. Perhaps someone like a deputy, a professor, or an MIT student? As Mary watched the reporter demonstrate the necessary steps, they didn't strike her as terribly sophisticated. Maybe someone with a basic understanding of technology could do it. If that was the case, you wouldn't need a PhD to accomplish what the kidnapper had done.

She examined the photo again.

How she'd hoped the proof-of-life photo would lead them directly to the kidnapper and Betty. That hadn't happened, and it might not, regardless of the level of searching and scrubbing the tech did.

That meant they'd have to find Betty another way. Mary was good at old-fashioned track-down-each-clue-and-put-them-together investigations. So was Chief McArthur. Together they would find Betty.

Since it was almost nine, Mary pulled up Eleanor's number. Maybe Eleanor had heard more about how to deliver the ransom. Now that the kidnapper had provided proof of life, he would want his money, and they needed to be prepared when he called.

Eleanor picked up after several rings. Mary could almost imagine her waiting for a nod from whoever was monitoring the phone to get approval that the machine was prepared to record the call before she answered.

"Hello?"

"Hi, Eleanor. This is Mary."

"Mary, you should call my cell, so we can keep the home line open for the kidnapper. He could call any minute." Worry threaded Eleanor's words together.

"You're right, so I'll be quick." Mary took a quick breath. "Have you heard anything from the bank? Is the money ready for the ransom?"

Eleanor hesitated. "My banker called first thing this morning and said they're still working with the police to get everything ready. I'm concerned they might not finish in time."

Mary chewed her lower lip as she took in Eleanor's words. "We'll have to pray they do."

"That's the thing." Eleanor blew out a breath. "The kidnapper just called—right before you did—and demanded more money. This time he asked for ninety thousand dollars. Said we needed to pay for making his life complicated."

"What? Ninety thousand dollars?" That was almost double the original amount. Mary fought against the tears that threatened to slip from her eyes.

"He wants the ninety thousand dollars by noon. And to think my banker had the fifty thousand dollars ready." Eleanor sighed. "The bank is working, but it's significantly more. I don't know if we can do this, Mary."

"I am so sorry for the position you've been put in, Eleanor." Mary swallowed to hold back the tears. "I am so sorry and so, so grateful."

Eleanor was quiet for a moment. "I appreciate that, and I want you to know I'll continue to do whatever it takes to get Betty back." She cleared her throat. "But now the bank has to mark forty thousand dollars more in small bills. And of course, the Ivy Bay bank isn't used to situations like this." She paused again, and Mary worried for a moment that Eleanor was having second thoughts. "Mary, what if I give the ransom to the kidnapper, and he disappears without letting Betty go?"

Mary wanted to argue that wouldn't happen. Surely the kidnapper had no interest in Betty beyond the financial reward. Doubt lingered, though, because Eleanor was right. Mary had read too many books, fiction and true-crime dramas, to know it didn't always go well. And this kidnapper seemed to be escalating with his changed demands and threats.

"I have to trust that if we do what he wants, this will end well," Mary said. "Even if I know that's naive."

After a moment of silence, Mary could almost see Eleanor's nod. "I've read too many of those books you love to pretend otherwise. I wish we could guarantee I'll get the money back. I know everyone thinks I have a lot, and I have been blessed. But it's not easy to access funds. They aren't as liquid as the kidnapper thinks."

Mary bit back the words that leaped to her tongue. The words that said Betty was irreplaceable and money wasn't. Yet she could easily imagine the hard position Eleanor found herself in. There was no question Eleanor loved Betty, and the fact she was working with the bank demonstrated just how much she loved her sister-in-law. At the same time, Eleanor found great comfort in her bank account. Releasing her money for a ransom was a risk, one Mary couldn't take lightly. "The police will do all they can to retrieve the money. If anything goes wrong, I promise I will do all I can to repay you. You have my word, Eleanor."

"I appreciate that. I'll just trust the police will reclaim it for me." Eleanor sighed, her voice weighted by shared but unspoken worries and fears. "This whole situation is a nightmare.... What must poor Betty be experiencing?" There was a rustling as if Eleanor were shaking her head to clear her thoughts. "I'll keep calling the bank. Owen Cooper has assured me he's working with a big Boston bank to make sure they do everything right as quickly as possible. I have to believe him."

"Me too, Eleanor."

"The good news is Chief McArthur thinks we can delay this awhile. Make sure we have everything in order with the bank. And it gives him more time to find Betty before we release the money."

"That is good news. Thanks again, Eleanor."

Mary hung up, her mind reeling with the full range of possibilities. She had read too many mysteries and could imagine scenario after scenario, most ending in ways she didn't want to consider. Too many of them illustrated what could go wrong after the ransom was paid. But what else could they do?

This time it wasn't a hypothetical book with made-up characters. It was her sister and their small town. It was real life. And she wanted it to end today. To have her sister home with her by nightfall.

With little more to accomplish at home and nervous energy pushing her to do something, Mary grabbed a bottle of water and crammed it in her purse. Then she grabbed the address she'd written down last night for Dr. Anderson's cabin.

Gus meowed in disapproval when she closed the front door in his face for a second day. If today repeated yesterday, she wouldn't know where she was headed from moment to moment and couldn't take Gus along. Whether or not he liked it, he'd be better off at the house.

Mary climbed in her car and pulled up her GPS. Dr. Anderson's address wasn't one she immediately recognized, but soon she followed the instructions on where to turn. The drive took her outside of Ivy Bay a few miles and toward a series of short roads that led closer to the cranberry bogs and then back toward the shore.

It was a journey of twists and turns, and she kept her gaze fixed on the rearview mirror as much as the road. After last night's note from the kidnapper, she had started to worry she was being followed.

The gravel road lined with large trees suggested the professor liked his privacy and solitude. This area was the antithesis of Boston. The road ended at a small cabin that looked more like a shack than a home. It was the kind of place that might warrant a little more time at Home Depot or Lowe's, or, Mary realized, the garden center. From her car, Mary noticed a patch of several dormant rosebushes. The sticks pointed toward the canopy of trees, devoid of any vegetation.

Mary parked the car but left it running as she climbed out. Something about the setting left her feeling that she wanted to be able to escape quickly if needed. The professor's red vehicle wasn't parked by the house, so it didn't look like anyone was home. Mary grabbed her cell phone anyway.

Mary eyed the trees that surrounded the home and its small yard. The shadows they cast converged on the house, sketching skeletal pictures across the wood siding. Two lawn chairs sat in front of a fire pit filled with ashes and half-burned logs.

Gathering her courage, she approached the house. Just because Dr. Anderson's car wasn't there didn't mean someone wasn't lurking inside.

A rough walkway of gravel led to the cabin's door. The windows on either side were shielded by partially closed curtains. During a slow walk around the small house, Mary peeked into each window but couldn't tell if anyone was inside.

There was only one way to know. She had to knock on the door.

The wind howled through the trees, snaking down her collar, and she imagined someone watching her from the shadows. She should knock, yet she felt rooted to the ground.

What if Dr. Anderson was inside? If he was the kidnapper, he wouldn't welcome her intrusion. But if he was home and if he could help her find Betty, then she had to know.

She gathered her courage and approached the door. She sneezed as she passed the rosebushes. The branches were dusted with a white powder. Could it be one of the products Dr. Anderson had bought at the garden center? Maybe he really was just a professor with a cabin to escape the city and his job.

Questions filling her mind, she lifted her hand to rap on the door.

A crash sounded inside, and she froze.

NINETEEN

❖◆◆❖

Mary's heart leaped into her throat.

"Betty? Betty?" Mary leaned into the door as she rattled the doorknob. It refused to budge. She slammed her fist against the door again and again. "Please let me in! Betty, I'm here!"

She held her breath as she listened, willing another sound, anything, to reach her.

All she heard was nothing but silence.

She stepped to a window and peered through it but saw nothing but a slice of beige wall. She tried to raise the window, but it was locked in place.

Mary rushed to the window on the other side of the door and tried to open it as well. When that didn't work, she cupped her hands around her face and pressed her nose to the dirty glass. All she could see was a rag rug of some sort.

When she reached the windows on the back of the cottage again, she jumped at a movement in the window. Then a cat hopped up on the window ledge, and she almost laughed with hysterics. The cat ignored her as he stared outside. When she cupped her face to the glass, he hopped down, and she could barely make out a broken glass on a counter.

She tried to shove the window open, but it, too, was locked in place.

Her breaths turned into gulping sobs.

Betty wasn't there.

She slid to the ground, trying to catch her breath and still her thoughts, but failed. She felt as though the threads of reality had unraveled along the edges. She so dearly wanted to find Betty that she'd imagined her sister trapped inside this cottage. Instead, it was just a cat.

Father, please help me. The prayer repeated in an intense chorus. *Be with Betty. Please keep her safe.*

As Mary's breaths slowed, her thoughts cleared.

So she'd heard a crash and found a cat and a broken glass. That didn't mean Betty wasn't inside. It just meant Mary hadn't seen any evidence to confirm it. Had she expected a sign on the door welcoming Betty to her home away from home?

Mary still didn't know whether Dr. Anderson was involved or simply had a tendency to show up at the same places she did. After one more walk around the house, she returned to her still-running car. After she sank into the driver's seat, she dialed the chief, but the call went to voice mail.

Mary headed back to Ivy Bay and her bookstore. As she waited for Sam's Seafood to open or the chief to return her call, she could at least check on the store and see if anything had come up yesterday she needed to address. Normally, Rebecca would call if anything needed her attention, but with the strange twist of events, Mary wouldn't be surprised if her assistant had avoided calling.

After she unlocked the front door, Mary walked inside her bookstore. As the sunlight streamed through the large front window, she felt a sense of homecoming in the peace that always filled the store before it opened. The act of unlocking the door made it feel like any other day. A normal day. One where once the store opened in a few minutes, it would be filled with the pleasant routines of customers exploring the bookshelves for just the right book, or the simple pleasure that came with each shipment of new books.

She loved the peace that surrounded her in her shop and the joys her job provided.

Sadness soon pushed the peace of the shop from Mary as she realized Betty could not stop by for a spontaneous visit. Even here, she felt Betty's absence in a deep sense.

Mary sighed and slipped her purse in a cubby under the marble-topped display case. Inside the case, there was an empty spot suggesting one of her prized first editions had sold. Later, she'd follow up with Rebecca and see who had splurged. She loved learning who valued the old books as much as she did.

Mary checked next to the computer and on the counter but didn't see any notes from Rebecca. She walked through the store and saw that everything was tidy and the beverage area was restocked, all ready for whoever wandered in during the day. Then she reached the back room where she had placed a love seat from her home in Boston and a small refrigerator and microwave. A mirrored medicine cabinet hung over the sink.

The only thing out of place was a box of books, which must have arrived yesterday. On a normal day, Rebecca would enter the books into inventory as they arrived, but with only one person in the shop, Mary wasn't surprised to find them left in the box on the love seat.

Mary ran her hand along the top of the box. It was comforting to know that the normal routines still occurred at the shop in a day that had otherwise been surreal. Customers bought priceless books, and Joe delivered still more with which to stock the shelves. It was the perfect cycle of a healthy bookstore in a thriving community, and she treasured it.

She wiped away a tear that had escaped, then grabbed a box opener from the small closet where she kept supplies. Maybe Rebecca had guessed the normalcy of checking an order for completeness would be a comfort for Mary at such an unbelievable time.

Mary opened the box and saw a collection of suspense titles waiting. Several had kidnapping themes, and Mary took a moment to reflect that when she'd placed this order, she'd never imagined how her life and Betty's would mirror the books' plots.

As she carefully checked the books against the packing slip, Mary took comfort in doing such a routine task on such an unusual day. After confirming the order complete and ready to enter into inventory, she stacked the books and carried one pile to the counter. In another normal routine, she jotted a note and stuck it on top so Rebecca would know they were ready to enter. Then she returned to the back room and grabbed another stack of books.

Once all the books were piled next to the computer, she knew she needed to return to her search for answers. If she didn't, the routines of her shop would fill her day and keep her from helping find Betty.

She grabbed the phone and dialed the chief's number. She tapped a pen against the countertop as she waited for him to pick up. She needed to know if he'd stopped by Jonathan Anderson's cabin again last night, and if he'd learned anything that related to Betty. Or maybe he hadn't returned her calls this morning because he was in the middle of a big break in Betty's case and didn't have time to stop.

That thought had her ready to end the call when it kicked over to voice mail. She left a short message asking him to call when he could, then tapped the phone against her chin. Maybe she should call Deputy Wadell. Chances were good he knew everything Chief McArthur did and could update her. If that call turned over to voice mail, then she'd have to wait for them to call.

"Hello?" Deputy Wadell sounded distracted, even distant.

"Deputy, hi, this is Mary Fisher. I couldn't find Chief McArthur and wondered if you could update me on Betty."

His sigh seemed exaggerated, as if she had somehow pushed him over the edge. He must be putting in lots of extra hours, because he was usually polite and patient. "He went home to clean up before we get ready for the ransom drop. I'm at Eleanor's until he gets back."

"So the kidnapper called again?" A spike of hope went through Mary.

"Not since the call raising the ransom amount, but I hope he will soon. Until then, there's not much happening. Unfortunately, kidnappings often follow this pattern of agonizing waiting punctuated by spurts of action. We're not even getting calls to the tip line. We need the kidnapper to call back if he wants his money today." He took a deep breath, and she heard the *whoosh* when he released it. "I heard about the earring at your house last night. Are you all right?"

"Yes. It shook me, but I'm fine." She forced lightness into her words, hoping he'd believe she hadn't driven that morning with an eye on her rearview mirror. "Has the tech found anything on the photo?"

"I wish she had, but she's not a miracle worker. I wouldn't count on getting anything off that photo in time to matter." His words bit into her, snapping one of her few threads of hope. "I'm sorry, Mary. She's done all she can here, and now we have to wait for the Boston lab to make time to analyze it. I hate to be blunt, but to them, this is a small crime."

Mary rubbed her temples. "You mean Betty isn't a priority to them?"

"No."

The word caught her off guard even as she knew he was right. Mary wanted to believe Betty was as important to the rest of the world as she was to her.

There was a moment's quiet. "I'm sorry, Mary, but I don't want to give you false hope."

"I understand."

"Look, have you talked to Eleanor today?"

"Not long ago."

"You've got to make sure she has the ransom ready when he calls." His words were muffled as if he'd put up a hand to shield his voice from others.

"It sounds like she's doing all she can."

"Mary, she's ready to stand firm and dare the kidnapper not to release Betty first. I don't like the idea of playing with Betty's life. It's just money."

But it didn't sound as though it was just money to Deputy Wadell. There was something in the way he said the words that made Mary wonder why he was so adamant about the ransom. Did it have anything to do with the kidnapping she'd read about the prior night?

"If this was my wife, I would want to do everything to get her back safely."

Could it be that all the times Deputy Wadell had been surly and uncooperative yesterday, he'd placed himself in the position of wondering what would happen if his wife was the one taken? That was something for Mary to consider. Mentally, he could be returning to that earlier crime and all that had gone wrong. The kidnappers had argued that the victim would have lived if they'd received their ransom when they'd asked. Their claims hadn't swayed the jury, but they did cause Mary to reconsider.

"Are people searching this morning?"

He sighed, a heavy sound. "They're starting to cluster. I'm still concerned the search could be a fool's errand. What if we need their help later and they feel like they've already done their part?"

"I don't know. Ivy Bay's citizens and our friends are the kind to stick by us through thick and thin. This is definitely a thin period." Worse than anything she'd experienced, and thinner than when one of her ice-cream experiments failed to firm up and freeze. "How can I best help today?"

"Stay close to your phone. We'll call the moment anything happens."

"All right. I won't come to Eleanor's unless you need me."

"All we need is for her to cooperate as soon as the kidnapper calls. At that point, we might not have much time to react and plan."

"Thank you, Deputy."

Mary ended the call and sank onto a stool behind the counter. Deputy Wadell's behavior the last two days was erratic, unlike his usually calm and unruffled demeanor. True, Betty's kidnapping was the first in Ivy Bay in a long time, but he was a professional, even if he was quite young. He was acting out of character, and that meant she needed to poke around and find out if there was more to it than the earlier kidnapping. Maybe the cause was unrelated to the kidnapping.

Either way, that was something she could do.

TWENTY

———◆◆◆———

A knock at the door of the bookshop pulled Mary's head up from her notes. Henry knocked on the door again.

She smiled as she pushed off the stool and headed to the front door, grateful to see her stalwart and steady friend. He'd been a rock for her since the first word of Betty's kidnapping. She sensed she'd need that steadfastness even more today.

As soon as she pushed open the door, he brushed past her. "Why didn't you call me this morning?" Fire smoldered in his eyes as he moved into the store.

"I didn't want to bother you if you had business to take care of or were getting your tire fixed."

"Mary, I told you last night that I was here for whatever you wanted. Besides, it doesn't take long to get a new tire. I've got my car gassed up out front, so I'm ready for whatever you need."

She walked back around the counter and sank onto the stool. "I stopped at Dr. Anderson's cabin this morning, but he wasn't there." She explained what had happened, and Henry stared at her.

"Why didn't you call me?"

Mary traced a pattern on the display case. "It was foolish. The minute I got there, I felt nervous, but I couldn't leave before I'd tried."

He reached for her hand. "Promise me you won't do that again. Not until we have Betty back. Please."

"I promise." Mary clicked on her cell phone and showed him the Sam's Seafood receipt. "It dawned on me as I looked at this last night that Betty wouldn't order this dish."

Henry studied the image for a moment. "You're certain?"

"Positive. She isn't fond of spicy food. There are so many dishes she loves at Sam's that I can't see her purchasing this one. She would have been concerned about the heartburn or other effects she might experience later."

"So we go to Sam's."

Mary nodded. "As soon as they open."

Henry pulled up his sleeve and looked at his watch. "That's in about forty-five minutes." He glanced at her. "Where do you want to go before then?"

"I don't know." She glanced at the list of places the deputy had been and the things he'd said. "Do you know the Wadells well?"

"Not too well. Why?"

"Deputy Wadell seems to be under extra stress right now. Any idea what's causing it?"

Henry shoved his hands deep into his jacket pockets. "That's an interesting thing to ask. Care to share your reasoning?"

"He hasn't been acting like himself on this case." Henry quirked an eyebrow, and she hurried on. "Yesterday he was very anxious while photographing the car, and he was against

Ivy Bay residents organizing a search, though he gave in eventually and helped. He's seemed very distracted and keeps taking furtive phone calls. Now he just told me to pressure Eleanor to pay the ransom as soon as the demand arrives. It makes me wonder why." She shrugged. "I've known Deputy Wadell for a couple of years. He's always been the perfect professional. On this case, he isn't."

Henry scratched behind his ear. "Maybe he feels too close to Betty. It could cloud his judgment. Maybe it's clouding yours."

"I won't deny that. It's different working a puzzle with these stakes. I learned last night that the deputy worked another kidnapping that didn't end well."

"There you have it. Nobody would want to work a kidnapping if an earlier one had ended in tragedy."

Mary nodded. "You may be right, but I'm going to slip across the street and check something. Can I meet you back here in ten minutes?"

"All right."

The front door popped open as they reached it, and Rebecca Mason flew in, her brown hair pulled back in a loose ponytail. "Mary! Oh, I am so sorry. It's been a crazy morning already, but I promise I'll get everything open and ready in no time."

"You're fine. Henry's the only one who's come by so far." In fact, now that she thought about it, she hadn't noticed much traffic on Main Street. She filed the thought away as she accepted a hug from her friend. "We're leaving, but I checked those books against the purchase order. They're ready to enter into inventory, if you have time."

"I'll make it a priority." Rebecca hung up her stylish coat, then turned. "Any word?"

"No."

Her friend's face fell. "I'm so sorry, Mary. I'm praying for Betty."

"Thank you." She cleared her throat. "I have my phone if you need me. Don't hesitate to call."

Rebecca nodded, but her attention was already focused on coaxing the computer to life.

Henry opened the door for Mary, and she followed him onto the sidewalk. "See you in a few minutes, Henry."

With quick steps, she turned down Meeting House Road and crossed to Cape Cod Togs. The store was one of Betty's favorites and a place she bought many of her classic and stylish outfits. It was possible Betty had stopped in the store sometime on Tuesday morning.

Today, Mary's purpose focused on determining whether Annaleigh Wadell was working. If not, she'd reconnect with Henry and head toward the restaurant. If the young woman was working, then Mary would take a little time to see what she could learn about the stress Deputy Wadell was under. Annaleigh might not know anything or feel free to talk about it, but the only way to find out was to pose the questions.

A pantsuit was paired with a floral dress in the store's large display window. Mary entered the chic store and paused to allow her eyes a moment to adjust to the interior of the shop. The cherry floors gleamed as soft light radiated from recessed fixtures. Clothing lined the walls in an uncluttered manner, and the racks on the floor were well spaced. The soft scent of eucalyptus, tinged with mint, mixed with the peaceful strains of string music to create a relaxed and soothing ambiance. A couple of upholstered chairs sat in a conversation collection near a trio of mirrors. Mary had waited there on a visit while Betty had a dress fitted. The shop's tailor had done an amazing job sizing the garment so it fit perfectly.

Mary swallowed around the sudden emotion in her throat at the memory and glanced around the shop.

"I'll be with you in a moment," a voice called.

A bit later, a woman in her midtwenties stepped from the back room. She wore a muted plum sheath that skimmed her form, and she'd topped it with a tasteful scarf that made her dark shoulder-length hair glow with richness. Her smile didn't quite reach her shadowed eyes, and dark circles suggested she hadn't slept in a couple of nights.

Mary saw recognition flash across the woman's attractive features. "Oh, Mary, how are you doing?" Annaleigh stepped toward her as if to hug her but stopped short of doing it.

"As well as I can."

"What can I do for you? Shouldn't you be out somewhere searching for Betty?"

"I am, in a way." Well, in more ways than one, but Annaleigh didn't need to know the full scope of her search. "Did Betty happen to stop in the shop on Tuesday?"

Annaleigh's brow furrowed as she studied Mary. "I only worked part of Tuesday. Bobby and I had an appointment in the afternoon."

"What about in the morning?"

"Sorry, I hadn't thought about that. There's been a lot going on at home." Annaleigh walked behind the counter and opened a book. "I don't remember for sure, but if she did, I would have noted it in here. We leave messages for each other about our best customers. Betty has a couple of pages in here." She flipped pages, then settled on one. "Oh, that's right." She pointed at a notation. "She slipped in for a short visit. Said she was looking for a gift." Annaleigh shrugged. "Whatever it was, she didn't find anything."

"About what time was that?"

"Right after we opened. We didn't have many customers Tuesday morning. Those we did have were like Betty. In and out in a few minutes." She shrugged and closed the book. "Wish I could offer you more."

"You've given me another piece of her day." Mary paused. "Is everything okay?"

"It will be. When Betty comes home, Bobby will be able to relax. It's too much like an old case."

"I read about that last night."

"He still dreams about that one." Annaleigh sighed, then chuckled wryly. "But if you really want to help, do you know anyone with about one hundred thousand dollars?"

Mary started at the number.

Annaleigh smiled innocently. "I know it's nothing compared to what you're dealing with right now. In fact, it's not bad. It's more like we're in limbo."

"To the tune of one hundred thousand dollars?" Mary tried to keep her expression and posture even.

"Well, we made an offer on a house, and it was accepted. You know how challenging it can be to find something affordable around here. Everybody wants to be from Cape Cod." A small smile flitted across her face. "I guess we do too."

"An accepted offer is good."

"Except the bank keeps changing the terms of the loan. We were good, then we needed an extra fifty thousand dollars, and now it's almost one hundred thousand dollars! We could lose the house. There's a backup offer, so the sellers don't need us anymore." Her expression fell. "The cottage is perfect for us. There are two extra bedrooms." A soft blush colored her cheeks. "We're ready to start a family, and this house would be the perfect place to do that."

Mary was stunned but knew she had to say something. "How much time do you have?"

"Just until tomorrow. Have you ever tried to raise a significant amount of cash in three days? Especially when the bank keeps changing what they want?"

"That is frustrating."

The young woman nodded. "Monday our real estate agent called. At Tuesday afternoon's meeting, the bank confirmed their final terms and deadline."

The store's door opened with an electronic ding. Mary bit back her next question as she saw Annaleigh break into a real smile. Before she could say a word, Mary knew Deputy Wadell must have entered.

"Hey, honey. Have good news?" Annaleigh said.

Mary turned as Deputy Wadell strode to his wife. He leaned down and kissed her forehead, then shook his head. "Sorry, nothing yet."

Annaleigh leaned into him. "Something will happen."

Deputy Wadell glanced at Mary and tipped his hat, but something in his expression made it clear he needed to be alone with his wife.

Mary nodded and backed toward the door. "Let me know what happens with the house. I hope it works out for you."

When she reached the street, she looked back inside and saw Deputy Wadell and Annaleigh engaged in what appeared to be an impassioned conversation. Lots of gestures and intensity.

Could the similarity of the terms of Deputy Wadell's home loan and the terms of the kidnapper's demands be a coincidence? As much as she wanted to believe they were, the numbers were shockingly similar.

It seemed impossible, but as the evidence continued to stack against him, Mary's suspicion of Deputy Wadell continued to grow.

TWENTY-ONE

———◆◆———

Mary had just crossed the street and returned to the door of her bookshop when Henry hurried toward her and took her arm. "Margie called and said we needed to head to the church. Something's happening there."

Mary glanced at her watch and noted that Sam's opened in twenty minutes. "Why?"

"Not sure. She just said to come by."

"I guess we have time to see what's happening."

Henry and Mary walked across the street to the church. When they arrived, Henry pointed toward the parking lot. "It's rarely that full."

"Could all those people be here for Betty?"

As she took in the activity, Mary stumbled to a stop on the sidewalk. The parking lot held a stream of people. Someone had even set up a tentlike covering to provide shelter from the cold. A few tables were surrounded by folding chairs, though they were sparsely used. Instead, people seemed to come in and out of the church basement. Cars filled the edges of the parking lot and spilled onto the sides of the road.

"There must be fifty people here."

Henry shook his head. "I think it's more. Margie mentioned that Pastor Miles told everyone to come here because the crowd had become a fire hazard at Bailey's."

"Oh my." Mary's words lingered in the air. A moment later, she was spotted.

"There you are." Jill Sanderson hurried toward Mary, the young blonde tightening a red scarf around her neck. "Dorothy sent me out here to watch for you. She seemed to know you'd arrive soon."

Mary looked at Henry, who gave an innocent shrug. Margie must have let Dorothy know. She turned back to her young friend. "I can't believe you're here."

"The boys are in school, and Grandpa is doing fine. I wanted to be here for you, just like you've been there for me so many times. If I don't get you in there, Dorothy will let me hear about it."

Mary followed her friend through the doors into the basement. So many times she'd been down here with Betty, celebrating events with friends, sharing meals, helping with service projects. Now everyone here wanted to help Betty. The hugs and gestures of sympathy as she made her way to the counter separating the main room from the kitchen overwhelmed her.

Mary bit back a grin as she noticed Dorothy directing Tricia Miles and Lynn Teagarden as they made coffee. Either woman could make it without assistance, but both graciously accepted the direction. As she watched the activity, Mary breathed a prayer of thanks for her wonderful friends who bore one another's burdens and idiosyncrasies.

"Mary Fisher. It's about time you got here." Dorothy approached and clasped her hands. "I haven't stopped praying for Betty and you."

Mary believed her. Dorothy could be demanding and focused on how she wanted things done, but she sure knew how to pray in a way that honored God. "Thank you. Thank you for all of this."

"I can't claim credit." The slim woman waved a hand in the air. "Someone else got everyone here; I'm just doing what I do best now that they're here. Much as I'd like to solve this mystery for you, I've learned you're better at the puzzles. But I can organize a group of people."

Johanna Montgomery hurried over from the other side of the room where she'd been interviewing someone. The head reporter for the *Ivy Bay Bugle* was one of Mary's favorite people. Her combination of kindness and integrity made her likable even when she researched and wrote about uncomfortable topics. "I never caught up with you yesterday. How are you doing?"

"All right." Mary settled on a chair Henry pulled out for her before he wandered to the coffee line. "I appreciate all you're doing to help spread the word about Betty."

"It's something a newspaper is good at." Johanna turned concerned eyes toward Mary as she sat down across the table. "What do you need?"

"Leads. I can trace Betty until she was kidnapped." The words felt so wrong. "Then she vanishes."

"And nothing helpful has come in?"

"Not that I know of, though Chief McArthur could better answer that question."

"When he's answering his phone again. Mrs. McArthur insists he needs a nap before the action kicks off again."

"He probably does. He's worked so hard since she was taken."

Johanna arched an eyebrow as she slid a paper across the table. "Here's today's issue of the *Bugle*. Betty's front and center with a picture, so hopefully that will generate good tips."

Mary took the paper and studied her sister's image. "Thank you. Where did you get her photo? I meant to get one to you."

"Pastor Miles gave me the one from the church directory. Let me know if you hear anything. Okay? Or if I can do anything?"

"If I can."

Johanna nodded, then stood to talk to a volunteer. Mary scanned the group crowded into the basement. So many dear friends and acquaintances filled the space, talking in clusters while they waited. Then her gaze settled on Jonathan Anderson against the far wall. Henry had wandered next to him, and they were talking.

Mary worked her way through the room, often stopped by friends, but she kept her eye on Dr. Anderson. He seemed to watch her progress too, and when she drew near, he said something to Henry, dumped his Styrofoam cup in the trash, and slipped up the stairs to the main floor.

Her hands curled into fists as Pastor Miles approached, preventing her from following Dr. Anderson. "Mary, can you believe what's going on down here? The phone rang all day yesterday. So many people love you and Betty and want to help that it reached a point we had to bring them here." He rubbed his hands together. "If we only knew how to use them."

"I'm so grateful, Pastor. But I thought Deputy Wadell was giving you ideas. He helped organize the search yesterday."

"He did. They didn't find anything yesterday, though. We've got enough people to do another search today, but the deputy doesn't have time to supervise." He shrugged. "Happens at a time like this, but it seems like a shame not to give all these people something constructive to do other than enjoying bad coffee together."

"Being together may be enough."

"Sure." He pulled something from one of the tables. "What do you think about sending people out in groups to post these along the main roads in town?" He handed her a black-and-white flier with Betty's church directory photo and information about who to contact if anyone had seen anything.

"This looks good."

"It's my version of needing to do something."

Gratefulness filled her at his kindness. "It certainly can't hurt to post these."

Pastor Miles smiled, then gestured to the stairs. "Why don't you say a few words, and then maybe we can break people up into smaller groups? Maybe Dr. Anderson can help with that."

"Why?"

"He had some great thoughts on how to do it efficiently when he got here this morning." Mary was unsure how to process that, and Pastor Miles spoke again. "How about it? A pep talk for the troops?"

"Yes, of course."

Pastor Miles clapped his hands to get everyone's attention. "Thanks for coming. Mary's with me and has a few things to share. Mary."

She stepped forward. "Thanks so much for being here. I just want you to know how much I appreciate you."

"You've been here for us, Mary," a voice in the crowd stated. Others nodded or affirmed the statement.

"Thank you. I don't know where Betty is, but God does. Please pray He'll keep her safe." Words fled as she looked at her friends. "Please keep praying."

"We haven't stopped, Mary." Margie's voice rose above murmurs of assent.

Kip Hastings chimed in from a table near the back. "I'm praying God will keep her safe."

The voices surrounded Mary with comfort, and she forced a smile as she recognized the sincere feelings behind the words.

Yet with each moment, each minute, each movement of the clock's hands, time passed. And with it the chance of finding Betty unharmed seemed to slip away.

Henry approached her. "It's eleven."

Another movement of the clock's hands.

"Sam's should be open," Mary said.

He nodded.

"Go do what you need to do, Mary." Pastor Miles placed a hand on her arm, a gesture that felt like a benediction. "We'll do what we can here."

Mary let Henry lead her from the basement and back into the sunlight. She lifted her face to the rays. *God, please let us learn something useful.*

"Amen," Henry said.

"I didn't say anything."

"You didn't need to." Henry walked beside her to his car where it waited in front of the bookstore. He held the door open until she'd settled in the seat.

"Thank you."

As Henry drove to the restaurant, she wondered if Sam's had a way to track the order number. If the guest paid in cash, would the server remember who placed the order three days earlier?

It took mere moments to drive to the restaurant down by the marina. One of the oldest in town, the building had started as a fisherman's shack but had experienced many incarnations until Sam turned it into a dive that was popular with fishermen and dockworkers.

Henry pulled his vintage car into the parking lot, and Mary sat a moment after he got out. It was more than waiting for a gentleman to open her door. It was more than the fear that the road would end here. It was the thought that somehow she would let Betty down.

Wherever she was, Mary knew her sister counted on her to solve this puzzle.

Henry opened her door, concern etching his face as he crouched at her level. "You doing okay?"

"Sure."

His gaze held her in place. "Really? I'm not someone you need to be polite with. I want the truth."

She met his gaze, letting him see the fear filling her. "I'm scared, Henry. I keep telling myself that God hasn't given me a spirit of fear, but that truth is being pushed out by the reality that I'm scared I won't find Betty."

"Let me pray with you."

Mary nodded as Henry took her hands. After he bowed his head, a moment of silence settled over them, sweet in its simplicity. "Father, I ask You to remind Mary that You are with her and with Betty. Lead us, guide us, and keep Betty safe. Amen."

The words were so simple, yet they soaked into Mary's spirit, calming her. "Thank you."

"I'll run an errand while you're in there. Call when you're ready, and I'll be back in two shakes."

"You sure?"

"Absolutely." He helped her out of the car, and she could feel his gaze on her back as she walked through the front door.

The low ceiling embraced her as she entered the vestibule where guests usually waited. The area was empty, but within moments, a server entered.

"Mary Fisher. You're the last person I expected to see here today." Andrew, the lead server, entered the room. In his red Sam's logo shirt and Dockers, he looked like any of the other waitstaff, though he'd been there at least forty years.

"I actually need a little help. Do you have a second to look at a receipt?" she asked.

"Of course."

Mary pulled up the receipt on her phone and then gave it to him. "I found this in my sister's car after she was taken. But there's an order for spicy crab, and she doesn't like spicy food."

"True, I remember that about her."

"Andrew, do you know if the person who served this order is here?"

Andrew shook his head. "She's not in, but she should be on her way. You can wait, if you like. I'd be happy to get you a tea, and it shouldn't be long."

"That would be great. Thank you."

He led her to a table where she could see everyone who came in and out. The restaurant was still quiet, but a couple of tables had occupants. Mary settled at the table to wait. She didn't want to accept more well wishes. Her brief time at the church had drained her.

After a few minutes, Andrew brought a woman in her midforties to the table. Mary had seen her a couple of times. Her bleached-blonde hair had black roots showing and was cut in a feathery mix that ended at her chin. Her smile was open and her expression curious.

"Mary, this is Lisa. She handled the order." Andrew waited as Lisa stepped forward.

"Hi, Lisa." Mary pulled out her phone and opened the photo. "I know it's a long shot, but do you happen to remember the person who ordered this meal?"

Lisa settled into the chair opposite Mary and studied the receipt. "Three days ago?" She blew out a breath that ruffled her bangs. "I've served a lot of meals since then. This one was toward the end of the lunch rush." Lisa tapped the phone against her chin, as if forgetting it wasn't hers. "Wait. You know what? I do remember this order." She handed the phone to Mary. "It was a young man. I'd guess college-aged. He wore an MIT sweatshirt. He'd *better* have been a poor college student because he didn't leave a tip. I never forget the people who stiff me out of a tip." Lisa leaned across the table toward Mary. "People seem to forget we live off our tips."

MIT? Young? Could it be? Mary didn't want to believe it, but she had to know if Lisa could confirm this college student was D.J. "Anything else you can tell me about him?"

"Other than that he was cheap?" She sighed. "He looked like a scarecrow. Tall, thin, and scraggly hair on top."

Mary clucked sympathetically. "Did he happen to pay with a credit card?"

"No, I remember he paid with cash, because he gave me a twenty-dollar bill, and I figured he'd leave some change."

"Was anyone with him?"

She shook her head. "Nope. He was by himself."

"What about what he ordered? It says it was extra spicy."

Lisa shook her head again. "That's not unusual at all for men. Many like the extra spice, though I'm not sure how they can taste the fish."

"Thank you." Mary smiled her thanks to Andrew and Lisa. "I appreciate your help."

Her heart sank as she slid from her chair and then walked across the dining room toward the door. She eased onto one of the benches where patrons waited and called Henry.

Lisa had described D.J. Was there any good reason D.J. would leave a receipt in Betty's car? Perhaps Betty had given him a ride somewhere? Perhaps it was totally innocent. Or was D.J. so desperate to pay tuition and fund his business idea that he would pull an unthinkable stunt on his own family?

Yesterday when she'd spoken to D.J., he hadn't mentioned going anywhere with Betty in her car, and he'd never struck Mary as the kind of person who could be that focused and cold-blooded.

Yet, if she was right, much as she hated it, then not only could he kidnap Betty, but he had.

TWENTY-TWO

A flash of sunlight off a car's windshield grabbed Mary's attention, and she looked outside and saw Henry stepping from his car. He'd want to know if she'd learned anything. What could she tell him? That the receipt suggested her cousin's son was involved?

She stood, but her steps dragged as she approached the door. She shouldn't overreact. It was entirely possible D.J. had been in Betty's car for any number of reasons, even if he'd failed to mention it. Why he'd been in Ivy Bay a day before his meeting with Betty was definitely confusing, but Mary didn't want to jump to conclusions, despite how easy it was reaching those conclusions.

Henry took one look at her as he held the restaurant's door open, and his mouth tightened. "How'd it go? Learn anything?"

"I did."

"That good?"

"Worse."

Henry opened the passenger door of his car, and she slipped onto the comfortable seat. He climbed into the car and then rolled down his window as Andrew approached.

Andrew held up a to-go bag as he shivered in his polo. "It's close to lunchtime, so I've got your favorites in here for you."

Henry accepted the bag with a grin. "Thanks, Andrew. That's very kind."

Andrew nodded and slipped back inside.

The aroma of fish and chips filled the car in all its fried glory. Henry opened the bag and peeked inside. He breathed in deeply, his chin tipped in the air. "Fish on a bun and chips in cups. We can eat while I drive. Where do you want to go next?"

"I don't know." Mary couldn't meet his gaze. The aroma of fried fish, a dish she often enjoyed, turned her stomach.

"I can wait while you decide." He waggled a fry in her direction.

"What if he did it, Henry?"

The fry stopped halfway to his open mouth. "Who?"

"D.J." She whispered his name, then repeated it with more force. "D.J. The person who bought the meal on this ticket is college-aged. Tall and thin like a scarecrow. He wore an MIT sweatshirt."

Henry turned to look at her. "Okay. It could be D.J. But remember, a thousand other young men around this part of the state would wear an MIT sweatshirt. Maybe it doesn't mean a thing."

"But how many of those young men know Betty and Eleanor? Are they each looking for money to start a business?" Mary didn't know many young men who attended MIT, but she knew one. And that one was looking very suspicious.

Before backing out of his parking space, Henry partially unwrapped his sandwich and took a bite.

Perhaps Jean could give Mary the insight into D.J. that she needed. She'd have to approach the subject carefully—her cousin wouldn't be happy with Mary's implications, but Mary would deal with that later. Right now, she needed any information she could find.

"I'll be back in a moment."

"*Mmm...*kay," Henry said, his mouth full.

Mary stepped from the car and away from the strong aroma of fried food. When she reached the corner of the parking lot near the marina, a stiff breeze blew off the water, and the air was tinged with the tang of salt and the call of seagulls.

Mary walked to the side of the restaurant that butted up to the fish market and leaned against a wall, sheltered from the wind. She pulled up Jean's phone number and waited for the call to connect.

The phone rang and rang, over and over. Was Jean home?

Mary expected the call to click to voice mail, when Jean picked up.

"Hello? Mary? Is there word on Betty?" Jean's voice was tight, almost strangled.

"No. Nothing's changed."

A huff of air brushed against the phone. "I don't know what to feel. Relieved? Upset?"

"It's hard to know."

"Is anything happening?"

Mary filled Jean in on the high points since they'd last talked.

"I wish I was there," Jean said. "I could at least wait with you."

"I'm not at the house much." Not any longer than she could help, because the strange emptiness pressed against her. "Besides, this will be over before you could arrive." Mary prayed that was true, then took a breath and plunged in. "Jean, I have an odd question for you. Has D.J. mentioned anything to you about needing money?"

"Not more than the average college student." Jean sighed. "I hope MIT is worth the cost. D.J.'s roommate, Connor, has the same struggles. His circumstances are much harder in some ways than D.J.'s, though."

"How so?" D.J.'s seemed hard enough for someone who wanted a great education from a pricey school and needed capital in order to put that education to use.

"His parents are embroiled in a nasty divorce. Sometimes I wonder if they've forgotten they have a son."

"That's too bad." Mary didn't know quite what to say next. "Well, I hope the degree is worth it for both young men."

"Me too." Jean exhaled. "Sometimes kids have to learn for themselves. I wish I could pay for D.J.'s school."

Now or never. Mary took the plunge. "Jean, can I be honest about something? I'm . . . I'm worried about D.J."

"Why?"

"Things seem to point to him being involved somehow."

"Involved? In what?"

"In Betty's disappearance."

Jean was silent, but Mary could feel the tension rising. "Mary, you can't be serious." Her words were sharp.

"I don't want to believe it, but—"

"But nothing. Mary Fisher, I'm disappointed in you."

"Jean, I wouldn't say D.J. might be involved without cause."

Cold silence responded.

"He was the last person to see Betty."

"You're sure?"

"He doesn't deny he had lunch with her."

Jean snorted. "Lunch is a far cry from kidnapping. Did anyone see him take her?"

"No."

"See?"

"Listen for just a minute, please."

"I'm not giving you any more time to tell me my son kidnapped my cousin!"

Jean was quiet a long moment, and Mary didn't know what to say. The uncomfortable moment extended so long that Mary wondered if her cousin had hung up without a word. Then she heard a whiff of air and held her silence.

"Do you have anything more?" Jean asked.

"Yes. He ordered a meal at Sam's Seafood on Monday. The day *before* Betty was kidnapped. And I don't understand why he would have been in town."

"How do you know that?"

"I have a receipt, which we found in Betty's car, and the waitress described a young man that looked just like D.J."

"Did he sign the receipt?"

"No, he paid in cash. And he didn't tip. That's what made him memorable to the waitress."

"D.J. always tips."

"Jean, you've made it clear money is tight."

"He worked as a server one summer and swore he'd always tip after that. There were too many times when he was left without even a dollar."

"That doesn't mean he tipped this time."

"What did he order?" Jean's voice was weary and burdened.

"Spicy crab with a baked potato."

"Could you repeat that?"

Mary repeated it.

Jean laughed, a nervous yet relieved sound. "And you're sure he was alone?"

"Yes."

"Then it's not D.J."

"It's not? How can you be sure?"

"D.J. is extremely allergic to crab. He wouldn't have ordered it. Within five minutes of taking a bite, he would fall into anaphylactic shock and be headed to the hospital if not the morgue."

Mary's breath caught. She was almost afraid to let it out. "You're sure?"

"I'm his mother, for heaven's sake. Yes, I'm sure."

A shiver of relief tore through Mary. She exhaled more deeply than she had in days. It wasn't D.J. *Thank You, Lord.*

"Mary, I'm not sorry it's not D.J."

"I'm not either, Jean. I never wanted it to be D.J."

"I know." Jean and Mary exchanged farewells, then hung up.

When Mary reached the car, Henry had the heater going full blast. "I was beginning to worry."

"I needed to talk to Jean."

"Learn what you needed?"

"No. Yes." She shivered and wrapped her arms around herself.

Henry frowned and pointed the vents in her direction.

"I'm all right, Henry. Just not getting any closer to figuring out who took Betty." She glanced at her watch and saw the hands sweep past noon. Another hour with no sign of Betty and little progress toward finding her kidnapper. She rested her head against the seat. "Are we going to find her?"

"Yes."

"I thought so. Then I talked to Jean...." She had to collect her thoughts, regroup, and move forward again. This wasn't the end of the search.

But if D.J. wasn't the one, who was?

TWENTY-THREE

◆◆◆

As Henry drove back to Grace Church, Mary pulled up the proof-of-life photo. Why couldn't she find a clue in the image?

No matter how she looked at it, all she noted was something peeking into the picture to the left of Betty. Try as she might, she could only tell it was wooden and thin yet sturdy.

What could she do with a nonitem like that?

At least now she had a description of the man who had dropped the receipt they'd found in Betty's car. She dialed Chief McArthur.

"This is Chief McArthur."

"Hi, Chief, this is Mary." She quickly filled him in on what she'd learned at Sam's Seafood about the receipt. "My cousin assured me her son couldn't be the person, even though he matches Lisa's description of the customer." She explained why.

"All right. I'll see what I can find out."

"Thank you. Any more calls from the kidnapper?"

"Not yet. Should be anytime. Keep your chin up, Mary. We'll get Betty back."

As she ended the call with Chief McArthur, Henry pulled into Grace Church's parking lot. He parked, then turned her way. "What now?"

"I'm not sure."

She really didn't want to mention to Henry that she was unsure of Deputy Wadell's behavior. What if she was wrong about him and his possible involvement? The last thing she wanted to do was color Henry's opinion of the deputy in a negative way.

Her phone rang, and she pulled it out, checking the caller ID. "Hey, Rebecca. What's up?"

"Hi, Mary. I hate to bother you, but there's been an odd delivery for you. With everything that's going on, I thought you'd want to know right away and be the one to open it."

"You're right." Mary opened the car door and started across the parking lot. "I'm at the church and will be there in a minute."

Henry hurried after her. "Need anything?"

"Can you see if Chief McArthur or Deputy Wadell are in the church or at the police station? If so, I may need them to meet me at the bookstore."

"Sure." Henry wheeled away from her toward the church, while she walked faster toward her shop.

Rebecca met her at the door, glancing over her shoulder at a manila envelope resting on the marble countertop.

"When did that arrive?" Mary asked.

"He brought it in." Rebecca pointed her chin toward the man who stood near a bookshelf filled with everything from Ian Fleming to Sue Grafton books.

"Dr. Anderson?" Mary said, stunned.

"Yes. He found the envelope on the sidewalk and brought it inside. He thought I'd know best how to reach you."

"Calling me worked."

"Faster than I imagined. I wasn't sure where you'd be."

Mary glanced at the professor, who had a novel open as he flipped pages without seeming to see or read anything. Was it too convenient for him to be the one to find an envelope addressed to her? He snapped the book shut, reshelved it, and then strode toward the counter.

"Mrs. Fisher, there's the envelope I found."

She studied the nine-by-twelve-inch envelope. Her name had been printed in block letters in black ink on the front. She pulled her gloves out of her pockets and onto her hands, then turned the envelope over. "Did you touch it?"

Rebecca shook her head. "I left it right where Dr. Anderson placed it and called you. I didn't want to do anything that could damage even the smallest clue."

Mary looked at Dr. Anderson.

"I had to carry it in but shouldn't have harmed anything." He held up gloved hands. "Should you touch it before the police arrive?"

"Henry's getting them, so they should arrive soon." Mary studied the back of the envelope. There were no marks that she could see. The envelope clasp was fixed through the small hole, but the closure hadn't been sealed or taped shut. Should she open it or wait for the police to arrive?

She sniffed the envelope, not sure what she hoped to find, but couldn't smell anything out of the ordinary. Dr. Anderson watched her with a slightly quizzical or bemused expression on his face, as if she were a subject in some experiment. She forced her attention back to the envelope. It seemed like regular paper, like any other manila envelope.

She loosened the clasp, and Rebecca took a step back, holding the shop's phone in her hand. "I'll just stand over here while you open that."

Mary released a tight laugh but kept her attention on the envelope. Two sheets of paper were inside, and she slipped them out. They looked like normal copy paper. With her gloves on, she couldn't feel it, but it looked ordinary. The words, however, weren't.

It was a note in the same block handwriting used in the note left on her porch along with Betty's earring.

Your sister is fine for now, but that can change if you don't quit looking for her. Tell the police to follow these ransom instructions exactly, or I will lose my patience. Delivery will be today at 5:30.

Dr. Anderson leaned closer, clearly reading the message. Mary flipped the page over but couldn't find anything else, such as where the delivery would occur. She fought the urge to slam her fist on the countertop. This kidnapper was taunting her.

She took a deep breath to still her trembling and turned to the second sheet.

I'm still okay. Please do everything he asks. Hang ten.
Betty

Mary expelled a breath. Betty was still all right, but "Hang ten"? Why would Betty use that phrase again? What was she trying to communicate? It was too odd of a phrase for her to use it without purpose, but Mary's search the first night hadn't turned up a thing.

"Should I call the police?" Rebecca's voice jolted Mary back to the moment.

Mary glanced out the window but didn't see Henry coming back with either the chief or deputy. "Yes, please call Chief McArthur." Mary rattled off his number while watching Dr. Anderson. "Can you explain how you found this?" she asked him.

"Certainly." He stepped back and pointed out the window. "I was walking past and noticed it leaning against the window on the small ledge out there. It was addressed to you, so I assumed you'd want it as quickly as possible. Since we've barely talked, I thought your employee would be better able to contact you quickly."

Rebecca murmured a few words into the phone, then hung up. "Chief McArthur said Deputy Wadell should arrive in a minute."

Mary hadn't noticed any eye movements or speech patterns that indicated Dr. Anderson was lying, but it still bothered her that of all the people in Ivy Bay, he was the one to find the envelope. It seemed too convenient.

"I'm grateful you brought it in," she said.

"Me too. Good timing."

"You've had a lot of good timing since Betty disappeared."

His face hardened, and she caught a glimpse of steel in his expression that hadn't been there before. "What do you mean?"

Mary took a steadying breath. She needed to be careful about how she proceeded. What if Dr. Anderson knew something that could lead her to Betty? "With so many people in the area, I just find it curious that you found it. There's so much traffic on Main Street I'd think it could have been any number of people."

"I was headed to a late lunch." He tapped his watch, as if emphasizing the time. "It's after twelve thirty."

"I thought they provided lunch at the church. Women were putting together sandwiches earlier."

"I'm not overly fond of sandwiches, so I thought I'd get my own lunch." He narrowed his eyes and met her gaze. "I don't have to help, you know."

"I do. So why are you? Especially when this is your break."

"Because I care about Betty."

"That's kind of you." She met his open gaze with a twinge of embarrassment. So far he'd answered all her questions. Would he continue to be forthright? "How did you and Betty meet?"

He turned to Rebecca and arched an eyebrow. "Is she always this inquisitive?"

"Kind of." Rebecca looked at Mary apologetically. "It's true."

Mary bit back a grin at the chagrin on her friend's face. Yes, she was curious and could be a bit suspicious when working on a puzzle. It was one thing that made her so good at chasing down the solutions. She had the ability to see things others sometimes overlooked—including nuances about the people involved in the mysteries. People like Dr. Anderson.

"I do appreciate your help, Dr. Anderson. I honestly didn't realize you knew Betty." Mary let the silence linger until Dr. Anderson shifted his weight and sighed.

"We met through mutual friends several years ago at a charity function."

"Oh, which one? Betty's involved in so many."

"I don't remember. It was so long ago."

Mary nodded, since she knew firsthand how easy it was for those kinds of events to blend together. "How did you learn to help with searches? You seemed quite knowledgeable yesterday."

"I study systems and what makes them work at MIT. Usually those systems are related to biology, but I've recently started researching a new system." He cleared his throat and broadened his stance. "Police investigations."

With his answer, Mary realized what attracted the professor to the search: He wanted to get out of the classroom and apply his ideas. And as she listened to his passion, she believed him. He really wanted to understand and improve the process.

"As I'm sure you're aware, time is of the essence with kidnappings. That means the systems need to work flawlessly to minimize harm to the victim. So I wanted to see if there was anything I could do to make the process of searching for Betty more efficient." He picked up a novel from a stack next to the cash register. "I've read enough of these to know how critical time is, and I don't want your sister to turn into another statistic."

"And your research can help?" Oh, how she wanted to believe it could.

"I think so, and learning from her case will help me better understand how this type of system works on a small scale. It's very different from the larger police departments like Boston."

"Have you learned anything that will help us find Betty?"

For the first time, he looked away. "It's too early, and I really focus on operations and processes." He turned back toward her. "But I'm still here and will be as long as I can help."

"Thank you." Mary tapped the envelope. "Did you look inside?"

"No. I brought it in the moment I found it."

Was he telling the truth? Mary considered his open expression and forthright answers. Any other scenarios seemed less plausible the more they talked. "Thank you for being honest."

"Of course. This has been interesting, but I'll see you ladies later." He handed Mary a card. "Here's my information if you have further questions." He nodded to Mary and Rebecca, then walked out the front door.

Deputy Wadell walked in after Dr. Anderson left. He tipped his cap toward them. "Mary, Henry said you needed me?"

"Dr. Anderson found an envelope outside and brought it to Rebecca." Mary gestured toward the envelope.

Henry arrived. "Who brought what in?"

"These notes." Mary pointed to the letters she'd left next to the envelope. "One's from the kidnapper, and the other is from Betty."

Deputy Wadell and Henry hurried over.

The deputy leaned toward the notes but didn't touch either. He pointed to one. "Is this Betty's handwriting?"

Mary looked closer, examining it for any discrepancies. "I think so. The signature is very similar. A few of the letters in the note itself seem a bit odd, but she would have been under immense stress. I suppose that could change her handwriting."

Deputy Wadell looked skeptical. Henry stepped toward the coffee and tea station. "Want anything, Mary?"

"No, thanks, Henry."

"And this one? Is the handwriting familiar?"

She turned back to the notes. "It looks like the same handwriting that was on last night's note. Can you take the envelope and letter so that someone can dust them for prints?"

"Sure. I'll do that right away. It would be nice if we found something, but you know it can take a long time to match a fingerprint if we find one."

"I know." It would at least be more than they had right now. If nothing else, they could use it to pin the kidnapping to someone if the person managed to slip away without being caught.

"So the professor brought the note in?"

"Yes."

"You think he might be involved?"

"I did, but now that I've talked to him, I don't know. Did you know he's consulting with the police department on the search?"

Deputy Wadell looked at her with widened eyes. "No. The chief would know for sure, but there's no reason to think he isn't."

"Do you know where Chief McArthur is?"

"Consulting with Boston and the state police. He's committed to finding Betty, if at all possible, before the ransom drop."

Why didn't Deputy Wadell include himself in that commitment?

TWENTY-FOUR

·◆·◆·

Deputy Wadell pulled on a pair of thin latex gloves and slid the letters into the envelope. "Did you touch the letters or envelope?"

"Not without these gloves on." Mary held up her hands, still covered by her driving gloves.

"How about you, Rebecca?"

The young woman shook her head. "As I told Mary, I left it where Dr. Anderson dropped it."

"Was he wearing gloves?"

"He said he was," Mary said, "so you shouldn't have to eliminate either of our prints from the envelope."

A minute later, Deputy Wadell carried the letters and envelope outside with promises to let her know if anything turned up.

Why was the kidnapper spending so much time telling her to back off from her search? Was she that close to finding Betty? And if she was, why did it feel like she had reached another dead end?

Mary pulled out a piece of scratch paper and jotted down the words of both notes. The kidnapper's block handwriting looked as unhurried and deliberate as the words. *"Your sister is fine for now."* She didn't like what the *now* insinuated. *"Tell the police to follow the ransom instructions exactly, or I will lose my patience."* Why wouldn't the police follow the instructions? Had the kidnapper watched too many TV shows or movies? *"Delivery will be today at 5:30."* At least that gave an indication of when this could all end.

Mary turned her attention to Betty's odd message. *"I'm still okay. Please do everything he asks. Hang ten."* The "hang ten" phrase was so unnatural...just as it must have sounded when Betty used it in that short call. It was not something Mary could ever remember hearing Betty say. There had to be a meaning behind it, or Betty wouldn't have used it twice in her two short communications.

Henry walked up with a mug full of black coffee. "Thought you'd want to know your cousin's son showed up at the church as I left."

"D.J.?"

"Yep."

Mary headed to the front door, wanting to see D.J. without the cloud of suspicion. "Call me if anything else happens, Rebecca."

"Yes, of course, Mary."

As quickly as the crossing lights allowed, Mary and Henry headed back to the church. What could Jean have told D.J. that would have him drive to Ivy Bay on one of his last days of spring break? "Did he say anything?"

"We exchanged a nod, and I followed Deputy Wadell back to your shop."

Mary bumped his shoulder and caught his smile. "You're a good man, Henry."

"Glad you think so."

"Not think so. I know so."

"So what next?"

"Say hello to D.J., then touch base with Chief McArthur and see if he knows anything about what Dr. Anderson said. I don't think he's involved either, but I need to confirm that he's consulting with the police. After that...we'll see."

As Henry held the door to the basement for her, Mary entered the church, her gaze searching the thinning crowd for D.J. She barely noticed that Henry didn't follow her into the building. Her cousin's son sat at a table near the coffee station, talking to Pastor Miles. When Pastor Miles saw her, he waved her over.

"Anything changed, Mary?" he asked.

She shook her head while glancing at D.J. He met her gaze, then looked down at his hands, which were clasped on the table in front of him.

Pastor Miles cleared his throat. "You know D.J.?"

D.J. looked up with a grin. "She's my mother's cousin, sir."

"Ah." Pastor Miles stood to give Mary a quick hug. "I'll leave you to catch up, then, Mary. I need to prepare Sunday's sermon." He stood and held his chair for Mary, then disappeared the moment she sank onto the seat.

"Mary." D.J.'s smile slipped, and he looked away.

"Hi, D.J." The poor kid looked uncomfortable enough that Mary suspected Jean had said something to him. "I'm sorry about my suspicions, and I'm so glad you weren't involved in Betty's kidnapping."

"It's all right." He shrugged. "I would have wondered the same things if I'd been in your shoes." He peeked up at her, and she could picture him as the awkward kid who'd never quite fit anywhere because his thoughts and dreams were beyond his age.

She reached across the table and squeezed his hand. "Thank you for coming."

D.J. shifted in his chair. "I'm sorry she's gone. Is there anything I can do to help?"

"I wish there was." She was grateful D.J. had come, even though he didn't know anyone except her. She was also so glad she didn't have to wonder anymore if he was involved in Betty's kidnapping.

She may have removed D.J. from her suspect list, but she wasn't any closer to finding her sister. Missing Betty was a physical ache that weighted her limbs when it overwhelmed her. It would root her to the chair if she didn't get up and do something.

D.J. cleared his throat. "Are you sure I can't do something?"

Mary nodded. "Being here is the best thing. Do you have your phone?"

"Right here." He patted his pocket.

"Good." Mary stood. "I'm going to keep looking for Betty. If I think of anything you can do, I'll call. Thanks for coming."

The basement door to the church banged open, and Susan Crosby hurried through. "Is Mary still here?"

"Over here," someone answered.

Susan pivoted and made a beeline for Mary. "You are a hard woman to keep up with. No sooner do you get to the bookstore than you turn around and take off again." She held out a pastry box. Mary took it with a shaky smile. "Go on, open it."

Mary inhaled slowly and then slid the lid up.

Two cupcakes were nestled inside, the scent of orange and chocolate escaping from the box.

"Two? I don't think Henry cares for cupcakes."

"You might be surprised." Susan smiled as she bounced on her toes. "Besides, one is for you and the other is Betty's."

Tears clouded Mary's vision as she took another look at the cupcakes, then slid the lid back in place. She cleared her throat. "Thank you."

"I locked the store to get this to you. Let me know if you need anything." Susan patted her arm. "Keep believing."

Mary nodded, but before she could say anything, Susan turned around and slipped away, leaving Mary warmed by the gesture of friendship.

Mary trailed behind Susan to the door. She kept her gaze on the box in her hands and all that the two cupcakes represented. As if by magic, the door opened in front of her.

Henry. Dependable, always-there-for-her Henry.

He followed her to his car, opened her door, and then walked around to the driver's side. She drew in a steadying breath and set the box of cupcakes on the floor behind her seat. She tugged out her phone.

"Where do you want to go?" he asked.

"Let's head out on 6A."

He turned the key in the ignition and eased out of the parking lot. While he turned onto Route 6A, Mary called Chief McArthur. He picked up almost immediately.

"Still nothing, Mary."

"Could you check something for me?"

"Maybe."

"Deputy Wadell probably told you about an envelope he collected at my shop."

"Not yet. What was in it?"

"A note from the kidnapper stating he'd have instructions for you for the drop at five thirty. And another from Betty saying she's fine. Maybe a kind of updated proof of life."

"All right. And you say Wadell took it?"

"Yes, he collected it and left about fifteen minutes ago."

"I'll follow up with him."

"Thank you." She rubbed her forehead. "What should I do now?"

"What we're all doing. We wait for the instructions." The chief sighed, the sound layered with exhaustion. "If the kidnapper wants the drop at five thirty, he'll have to call with location instructions soon. I promise I'll keep you posted."

"Thank you, Chief." After he hung up, Mary continued to stare out the window.

Henry tapped her on the hand. "So?"

"I don't know." Her mind was a complete blank on what their next step should be.

A commercial ended on the radio, and the DJ announced the call letters for one of Henry's favorite oldies stations. A new song started, and soon Henry hummed along to "Surf City."

"Remember this song, Mary?"

"Of course. It was so popular I would have had to live on an isolated island not to know every word."

She smiled and joined Henry in a slightly off-key harmonization. She started laughing until the words caught up with her. Wait a minute!

Surf City.

Surfing.

Hang ten?

TWENTY-FIVE

Hang ten.

Mary searched her memories. It was certainly a stretch, but this song *was* a favorite of Betty's and hers when they were young teens. Could Betty have been obscurely referring to this song?

She and Betty had played their Jan and Dean record continuously one summer. Betty had left the record at their grandparents' house, and in future summers, it had formed part of the soundtrack for their time in Ivy Bay.

But "hang ten" didn't appear in the lyrics. Why would Betty use that phrase instead of something else like "surf on"? Even then, a reference to a beach term felt like a stretch.

Betty was trying to communicate something to Mary. Was Mary supposed to remember something from their summers in Ivy Bay? If so, what?

As the blocks slipped by, Mary's mind pulled out images from their summers. She couldn't think of a time that "hang ten" was prominent. That had always felt like more of a West Coast phrase to her, though she supposed it was used anywhere surfers gathered.

What could a phrase that referenced the act of curling ten toes over the edge of a surfboard have to do with Betty's kidnapping?

As Mary mulled over what Betty meant, she decided it had to do with the beach. That focused her more than when she first heard the phrase Tuesday night. Even her research that night had left her struggling to find a connection.

"Henry, would you mind driving alongside the beach?"

"No problem." He turned at the next intersection and began maneuvering toward the shore. "What are you thinking?"

"'Surf City' made me think about Betty's strange use of 'hang ten.' I'm wondering if she was trying to point me to the beach. Maybe if we drive alongside it, I'll see something."

Henry executed another turn. Any number of roads ran along the coast. Roads with names such as North Shore Boulevard and Salt Marsh Road. Unlike California's Pacific Coast Highway, Route 6A wove along the contour of the bay but still a distance from the beaches.

"Am I crazy?" Mary whispered as she watched the car move onto smaller and smaller roads.

"I don't think so." Henry glanced at her before returning his gaze to the road. "It's worth a drive to see what we find."

Mary wasn't sure what she was looking for and prayed she'd know it when she saw it. If not, this was a wild-goose chase, but she didn't have anywhere else to look or a better idea.

What am I supposed to see, Betty?

As the roads led ever closer to the bay, Mary's thoughts wandered. Since she'd eliminated D.J. and Dr. Anderson from her suspect list, it meant she was down to Deputy

Wadell or someone new. Who could that new person be, if he existed? Whoever it was had to be connected to Eleanor or Betty somehow.

She ran over her conversation with D.J. What had he said about his roommate? That his family had a beach house? He hadn't called it a cabin. Had Connor heard something about D.J.'s family that made him . . . what? What would a kid with no connection to Ivy Bay have to do with the kidnapping? But he'd made an appearance at the diner Tuesday when Betty and D.J. were there.

Could Connor be involved?

Henry turned onto a road that fronted the deserted beach. "Know what we're looking for?"

Mary rubbed her temples as Henry kept driving. The beach outside the car was familiar. These were beaches she'd played on, waters she'd swum in, areas she currently walked. Nothing she saw explained why Betty would have used such an odd phrase.

Betty wouldn't have said it and then written it without a reason. One time had seemed odd, but the second use couldn't be explained away.

So where did that leave her?

Henry kept driving, turning on side roads and making sure he covered every piece of beach they could reach by car.

"People don't do much surfing on this side of the bay."

Henry tapped his fingers on the steering wheel. "I see some, but most of it is up toward Wellfleet and Provincetown. Otherwise people are on the Atlantic side. We're too sheltered in here for great waves."

"And if they surf, it's with those shorter boards, right?"

"Sure. But I've seen a bit of it all when I'm out with my boats."

If surfers used "hang ten," would one of their shops carry that name?

Her phone rang and she jumped, knocking the phone to the floorboard. She groped for it, the shrill sound jolting through her as she finally grabbed it. She barely registered the chief's number on the screen as she accepted the call.

"Hello?"

"Mary, I've only got a minute because the ransom instructions finally arrived."

"And...?"

"Six o'clock, so just a bit later than the note said."

Mary had no idea why the kidnapper was changing things so often. "Gotcha," she said. "Do you need me to come back and help with the ransom drop?"

"It's best if you don't. He asked for Eleanor."

"In the demand?"

"Yes. She's to drop off the money at one of the golf courses along the beach. He'll call with that information at five thirty."

"Thank you, Chief."

After Mary hung up, she called Eleanor. "How are you holding up?"

"The kidnapper wants me to deliver the money."

"Chief McArthur told me. Is there anything I can do to help you through this?"

"Other than give me a dose of your courage?" Eleanor's voice quavered on the last word. "I'm okay. I just can't wait to get my sister back."

Mary had never heard Eleanor call Betty her "sister" without tacking on the "in-law" part. The change touched Mary.

"So it's all happening at six o'clock."

Eleanor sighed. "I hope I do this right."

"You'll be fine, Eleanor. If you need anything, call me. Otherwise, I'll keep looking until Betty's home safe."

After she hung up, she realized Henry had pulled over and parked. "Why are we stopped?"

"Did you see anything around Ivy Bay?"

"No." Mary realized Henry had driven up and down the beach while she'd talked. "Nothing looked right."

"Or wrong."

"Correct."

"Do you want to keep driving?"

"Yes, let's head toward Boston since the police said the first call was within thirty miles of Ivy Bay. If we don't see anything along there, we can go up the other direction."

"All right." He got the car going, and Mary watched the scene flowing through the window.

The areas along the beaches were deserted, empty compared to how they'd look as the weather warmed and spring took hold, then turned to summer. Most businesses on the beach were boarded up in the interim. And none seemed to relate to "hang ten" or the lyrics of "Surf City."

Maybe D.J. would have an idea. She called him, and after a couple of rings, someone picked up.

"Hello?"

"D.J., this is Mary."

"Do you have something for me to do?" Eagerness laced his words.

Mary explained that she and Henry were looking for a location that could tie to surfing or the phrase "hang ten." "Can you think of anything like that around where you live?"

Silence followed her question, and she could imagine the intense look on his face that he wore when concentrating. His eyebrows would knit together over his nose, and he'd pinch his chin. He could get a singular focus when he wanted. "I can't. Sorry."

She deflated a bit. Why would she think there was any place near his part of the bay?

"I can go look, if it helps."

"Actually that would be great. Are you sure?"

"I'm wasting time sitting at the church. I'd rather do something useful."

"We're headed toward Sandwich and points west. How about you drive along the bay as it curves to the north?"

"Sure. What are you looking for specifically?"

Mary explained why she thought Betty was pointing to surfing with her "hang ten" comment.

"Sure that's what she was doing. Why else use that phrase?" D.J. said, chuckling. "I haven't heard anyone use it lately. So you want me to note the buildings with surf themes?"

"If you could." Oh, it sounded crazy when he put it that way.

"All right. I'll call you if I see anything."

"Thanks. Before you go, you said your roommate has a beach cottage, right?"

"He wouldn't call it a cottage. But yeah, his parents have one he talks about all the time. He says we'll go there, then backs out. Makes me wonder if it's real or another story he spins."

"What other kinds of stories has he told?"

"The usual things when you're trying to impress a new roommate with how important you are."

"I haven't had one for a long time."

"How much money your family has. The crazy vacations they've taken. That kind of thing. It'd be easier to believe if he could pay his rent and tuition. He's closer to getting dropped than I am. I can at least get student loans."

Interesting. "I know this is kind of a strange question, but do you know where his beach house is?"

"I'm not sure. As I said, I've never been, despite his big talk. Somewhere along the bay side. Relatively short drive from Boston, I guess."

"I've always wondered what locations people choose for their beach houses."

"Are you thinking about buying one, Mary? Maybe I'll come live with you."

She chuckled with him.

"Seriously, though, why all these questions about Connor and his beach house? Have you decided he could be involved?"

Mary bit her lower lip as she tried to think of how to answer.

"Wait a minute. You have." D.J. whistled. "You think because he was in Ivy Bay at the diner, he could be involved."

"It's possible."

"I don't know, Mary. Sure, he's stretched the truth a bit about his family's influence, but that doesn't mean he's a kidnapper."

"Can you tell me Connor's last name?"

"Hannon. Look, you don't really believe he was involved, do you? Who are you going to suspect next? Your friend Henry?"

Mary glanced at Henry as he drove down the highway. "Of course not. Look, D.J., if I can get some basic information, I can eliminate Connor from my list of people Betty had contact with on Tuesday. I know I'm stretching, but I'm out of ideas, and the ransom drop is at six. I'm running out of time."

"I guess that makes sense."

Mary breathed a sigh of relief. "Do you know his parents' names?"

"No. Neither comes around. For such big talk, his family seems to be falling apart."

"That's sad." She hated to see families destroyed by divorce.

"Yeah. He's not taking it well." D.J. paused as if embarrassed he'd said too much.

"Any ideas where they live?"

"Somewhere around Boston."

"Thanks. Be sure to let me know if you see anything while you drive." When she hung up, she put the phone away. "I'm not sure a last name will be enough to find the house."

"How do you want to do that?"

That was a great question. The house wouldn't be in Connor's name. She opened the browser on her smartphone and entered Hannon in the search field. It pulled up white page listings for more than one hundred people in Massachusetts and indicated there were hundreds more. However, when she entered Connor, his name didn't appear. She didn't have time to start calling random Hannons to see if one could be related to Connor. As she scrolled through the list of Hannons, many were in Boston or a surrounding community.

Henry kept driving the coast as she worked. Mary pulled out the notebook and began noting the names that might be relevant and their related addresses. None of those looked like they belonged to a beach house.

"We've been driving for a while, and I've got nothing," Mary said.

"Yet."

"*Yet.*"

She scanned her lists and notes while occasionally glancing out the window. She reentered "hang ten" and "Massachusetts" in her phone's browser but didn't see any businesses with that name as she scrolled the search results. Business owners seemed to think the bay was too protected, the waves too small for surfing to be a solid source of income.

It was now three o'clock. If they didn't see something by four, she'd insist Henry turn around and go back. She wanted to be close to Ivy Bay when the ransom drop occurred. She wanted to be ready to run to Betty the moment the kidnapper breathed a hint of where her sister was being held.

Her phone rang again. Chief McArthur.

"Mary, we've got something on Betty's location."

"You do?" She sagged against the seat. *Please, God, let this be something.*

"The e-mail was sent from somewhere in the area around Quincy."

"You're sure?"

"As sure as the best techs Boston PD has can be."

"Okay. It's still a large area but smaller than a thirty-mile radius."

"We'll continue to dig, but I wanted you to know."

"Thank you." She looked at Henry, who flashed her a grin before refocusing his attention on the road. She turned back to her conversation with Chief McArthur. "We're past Sandwich and headed toward Quincy now."

"Do I want to know why?"

"A crazy gut instinct." She turned to Henry. "Can we take 3A toward Plymouth?"

"Sure." Without questioning her, he adjusted the direction he was driving to take that route.

"Stay out of trouble and keep me posted, okay, Mary? I don't want anything to happen to you."

"I will. You get the ransom taken care of."

"Already on that." The chief sounded so tired.

"Any more information on which golf club?"

"Nothing. All he said was a country club near the bay. We've got police near the Ivy Bay country club and a few others. He's calling back at five thirty with the final location, and Eleanor will have no more than twenty-five minutes to get there."

"That might not be enough time depending on where he sends her. She could hit rush hour." Mary rubbed the bridge of her nose.

"Yep." The chief paused a moment. "Wadell and I have wrestled it to the ground. He finally convinced me the positives outweigh the potential negatives if we do it, but they flip if we don't."

"Deputy Wadell has seemed distracted and a bit erratic the last couple of days, hasn't he?" Mary took the opportunity to talk about him, since the chief had brought it up. It was the only natural way to ask questions.

The chief chuckled, a low sound. "He's in the process of getting a home loan. It's got him and his wife tied in knots. They haven't figured out that there isn't one perfect house yet. If they don't get everything arranged in time to get this one cottage, Wadell's convinced his wife will never be happy again. He's wrong. And he'll learn that eventually, but fortunately for him, the revised loan came through earlier this afternoon."

"That's great news!" Mary forced enthusiasm into her voice, even as she wondered if this meant she could clear Deputy Wadell from her suspect list.

"It is. I've already noticed him loosening up."

"Please pass along my congratulations." The chief agreed, and Mary studied the Sandwich Country Club as Henry drove past it. Was that the one the kidnapper would use? "Are you focused on the country clubs in the area the e-mail was sent from?"

"There have to be a half dozen in that area alone." The chief grew quiet. "We're doing all we can with limited resources, Mary."

"I understand." Mary kept her gaze on the businesses they passed. "I'll call if we find anything. We can check out some of the country clubs as we drive back to Ivy Bay. Thanks for letting me know about the e-mail." She hung up and processed the new piece of information. They had to be headed in the right direction.

Henry spoke up. "Good news?"

"Maybe. The kidnapper wants the money dropped at a country club but hasn't told us which one."

Henry whistled. "There are quite a few around the bay."

"And they narrowed the e-mail to having been sent from Quincy." Should she have D.J. turn around and head this direction? She decided she'd rather have him drive north and be certain she hadn't made a mistake in the direction.

The ransom drop would happen in a couple of hours.

Was the botched kidnapping years ago, combined with the house loan problems, enough to explain Deputy Wadell's strange behavior? Now that the loan had gone through, did that mean he wasn't a suspect?

"We've got until six, Henry."

"To find Betty?"

"If we don't find her by then, the ransom drop will happen."

"So we keep driving."

Route 3A rolled past as Mary considered the chief's comments about Deputy Wadell. She wasn't sure she bought the excuse of the home loan for his erratic behavior, but combined with the former kidnapping, it might explain everything. Maybe the chief was right that he would be back to normal now that the loan had cleared.

Somehow, she needed to know if Deputy Wadell still needed the ransom. Mary took a deep breath, then blew it out. If she was going to call, she needed to do it. She called Cape Cod Togs and was relieved when Annaleigh picked up.

"This is Mary Fisher. I wanted to check on you. You were so upset this morning."

"Aren't you sweet?" The enthusiasm in Annaleigh's voice made Mary cringe. "You wouldn't believe it, but the loan came through this afternoon. I'm so excited I can barely focus on the store. We can finally move out of our apartment and into the cottage. Good-bye, beige walls!"

"That's wonderful news."

"It couldn't be better. I'm so tired of our small space. It just doesn't feel like a home."

"Well, congratulations!" Mary shoved enthusiasm into her words even as she felt worse for doubting Deputy Wadell.

"We're thrilled. I think Bobby's as relieved and excited as I am. He's been by a couple of times since we got the word. We both can't believe we're getting our house after all." She giggled, then sputtered to a stop. "Listen to me. Any news on Betty?"

"No. Deputy Wadell would have shared it with you if there was."

"You'd think so, but he keeps a tight lid on work. Doesn't want to compromise investigations with even a hint of indiscretion. Can you imagine Bobby doing anything like that? That's not my husband."

Mary didn't mention how easily she'd imagined that scenario over the last two days. "I'm so glad the loan came through."

"Thank you! And thank you for praying. I was so blue this morning. I didn't see how it could happen. This feels like a miracle."

It did feel that way as Mary said good-bye and hung up. She couldn't begrudge Annaleigh her happiness at the good news. Still, she was ready for good news to celebrate about Betty.

If the loan ups and downs were the source of the deputy's odd behavior and strange calls, then someone else was the kidnapper. Someone she hadn't seriously considered.

The thought left her cold.

She'd cleared all her best suspects, leaving just one person: Connor.

If the waitress was correct that the person who placed the order for spicy crab was a scarecrow of a college-aged man, then could it be D.J.'s roommate, Connor? There must be a thousand college-aged young men in the Quincy area who would wear an MIT sweatshirt.

Where did that leave her as the minutes swept by toward six o'clock?

Connor matched the description, and it seemed he had financial need. But D.J. made it sound as though he hadn't said anything to Connor that would give his roommate knowledge of Eleanor's assets. Still, everything was beginning to point toward Connor.

Mary watched the beach. This one was as deserted as the rest, with a few brave seagulls twirling on air currents and a woman walking a large black lab down by the water's edge. A slow breeze pushed against the water. Scenes like this usually filled her with peace and gratefulness that she lived on this amazing stretch of coastline.

Another portion of beach slid into view, with a few dunes topped by dry grasses. Where the dunes slipped toward the beach, a small shack of a building sat between the dunes and the water. She squinted at it. It definitely wasn't a lifeguard station. They'd passed one of those not too long ago. No, it was something else.

She looked again, then squealed. "Henry, stop! Stop the car!"

Almost before he had it in park, she launched out of the vehicle.

She had to get closer and see if it was what she'd thought. Or were her eyes deceiving her, the hopes of her mind superimposing themselves over the reality standing in front of her?

TWENTY-SIX

M ary scrambled off the shoulder and toward the dunes. Her shoes slipped in the sand as she tried to climb one. Then she saw a path leading around them and angled for that instead. The path was sand that seemed to reach up and grab her shoes, but it was better than slogging uphill.

Henry chugged up beside her. "What is it, Mary?"

She pointed toward the shack. "Do you see that?" The words came out in short gasps.

"Yes."

"Is it what I think it is?"

"I don't know."

"The sign, Henry. What's the sign say?"

He squinted a bit as he looked that direction. "Surf City Snack Shack."

"That's it." Mary threw her arms around him and squealed. "We've got to be close."

"Close to what?" Henry held her firmly as if concerned the stress had gotten to her.

"To Betty. This is why she kept using the phrase "hang ten." She knew eventually I'd get that she was talking about surfing. A snack shack. Of course."

Mary studied the building. While it looked abandoned at this time of year, she seriously doubted Betty was in there. Still, she had to check. She couldn't be this close and not make sure.

She took off again across the sand, fighting for balance as she moved as quickly as she could toward the shack.

What had looked ramshackle from the road looked sturdy up close. The outside had been weathered by time and the sand, but she could tell someone took pride in the business.

As she approached, she started yelling. "Betty? Betty, it's Mary. Are you here? Please call out if you are."

When she reached the back door, she banged on it with all her might. "Betty?" She banged some more. "I'm here. Please be here." She hurried to the front and beat against the plywood covering the serving window.

Henry tried opening the door and examined the sand that had blown up against it. "I don't think anyone's been here for a while, Mary. Just look at how high the sand has blown against the door."

She knew he was right. She knew Betty wasn't here. In some ways, it would be a good place to hide someone. In other ways, it didn't make any sense. It was too close to 3A. Someone would have noticed activity at the shack and alerted the owner or police.

Still, Mary stood for a minute by the boarded-up window and prayed to hear Betty's sweet voice. Instead, she heard nothing except the shrill calls of the seagulls.

She pounded the plywood one more time, fighting back frustrated tears. "Okay, so if she isn't here, where is she? Why lead me here if this isn't the place?" She blew out a steady stream of breath, trying to focus her mind. "She used that phrase to communicate to me. I know she had to be careful since the kidnapper would see everything she wrote or hear everything she said."

"Yes," Henry agreed.

"So why lead us here?"

"Do we know this is the only one of these on the beach?"

She scanned the beach. A block or so away, cottages mixed with nice homes fronting the beach. "Let me do a quick search for Surf City." She pulled out her phone and scrolled through the search results. Nothing else with the name Surf City came up in the area. "Could it have been the last thing she saw before they reached their destination?"

"The kidnapper wouldn't let her give us an address."

"But she knew 'hang ten' would be enough to get me to 'Surf City' with the right prompts." She turned and looked up the beach in the other direction.

"What are you thinking?" Henry asked.

"Maybe she wanted us to know this was the right general location." She chewed on her pinky as she turned back and forth. Was she right? Desperate? Or a combination of both? How could she know?

The only method she could imagine was a door-to-door search, but most of the cottages would be empty. In a couple of months, the beach would transform with summer's warmth, but for now, it had an abandoned feel.

The wind picked up, and she shivered. *Okay, God, what next?*

Mary pulled her phone out to dial the chief, except her hands shook so much she kept fumbling the numbers. She took a deep breath and tried to settle her nerves. On the third try, she finally pulled up his number.

The phone rang and rang. Mary paced as she waited for the chief to pick up. "Come on, come on."

Why wasn't he picking up?

She needed to let him know what was happening. This could be their first big clue on where Betty was. If they could find her before the ransom drop, then all they'd have to do was find the kidnapper. Eleanor's money would never be out of their control, but most important, Betty would be back with the people who loved her.

When voice mail picked up, she left a message. "Chief McArthur, I think we've found the neighborhood Betty is in. Please call me."

She hung up and paced up and down the sand in front of the Surf City Snack Shack. What now?

Henry watched her as he leaned against the building in a relaxed position. She knew the moment she asked him to do something, he'd jump, ready to help in any way he could. Until then, he wouldn't pressure her or get in her way unless he had an idea.

A few hundred yards from Surf City, beach houses and charming cottages lined the beach on each side. Victorians and Cape Cod styles mixed side by side in a charming blend as far as she could see.

Which way should she go?

Mary could sense Betty was close, maybe in one of these houses or cottages. Time was so short. She couldn't afford to waste time in the wrong place.

Her head swiveled as she looked in each direction.

They looked the same. Beautiful beach homes of those who could afford to live on the bay.

She stopped short and blew out a breath. She had to choose. There was no way to know for sure which house Betty waited in, but they had to look. If they failed, the ransom drop would still happen.

Maybe the kidnapper would return Betty to them. But if Mary found her first, then this nightmare would end. They could go home and pretend the last few days were a bad dream that had finally ended.

"Henry?" He snapped to attention and looked her way. "Let's go west. See if we can find anything."

"Checking the houses?"

"As much as we can."

Adrenaline raced through her as a breeze kicked up from the bay. As the sunset grew closer, temperatures would only drop, making a search colder and more difficult.

Together they headed back toward the boardwalk and then along the edge of the beach toward the houses. As they neared the first house, a charming Victorian with multicolored gingerbread trim, Mary's phone rang.

She snatched it out of her coat pocket and swiped to accept the call. "Chief."

"Where are you, Mary?"

"Along the beach near a little snack shack."

Someone mumbled in the background for a minute, then the chief was back. "Why are you there?"

"I finally understood why Betty said, 'Hang ten.'" Mary kept moving toward the first house. "She wanted me to look for a location related to surfing. I just found a Surf City Snack Shack here near Sandwich."

Henry walked up the crushed seashell path to the home's front door. Mary watched him go as Chief McArthur sighed.

"I know we're close to the time of the ransom drop," she continued, "but could you send anyone to help us with the search? She's here, Chief. I know it."

"Do you know where specifically she is?"

"Not yet. But I'm going house to house."

"Mary, don't. Wait for—"

"Chief, I'm sorry. But this is my sister. I can't wait."

There was a brief silence. "I'll figure out how to get to you. And quickly."

"Thank you."

She hung up and then looked again at the proof-of-life image on her phone. The background was so neutral it didn't help them, and it was of the inside, so there was nothing to point to what the place looked like on the outside.

She squinted at the image, then expanded it and looked at it in segments. She'd done this several times since the photo had arrived but had never noticed anything helpful.

The wooden item in the background remained something she couldn't identify. Why couldn't there have been a piece of mail with an address? Or a photo of a family that someone could identify for them? Why did those coincidences only happen in books and movies?

"You coming?" Henry's words pulled her attention from the photo. "I really don't know what I'm doing other than trespassing."

Mary walked up the path toward him. "Let's look in the windows we can. If the homes are boarded up for the winter, we won't be able to see much. If we see anything that indicates someone's been around, we can note the address."

"And if we run into someone?"

That was the tricky part. How to ask about Betty without tipping off the kidnapper. There was still a slim chance the kidnapper wouldn't recognize her immediately as Betty's sister. She hadn't heard from the press, other than Johanna, and that wouldn't be printed until tomorrow.

"We could say we're looking for a place to rent over the summer."

Mary hoped the kidnapper was already away preparing for the ransom drop. Then they could look in peace.

At the sound of a car pulling alongside the curb, Mary tensed.

TWENTY-SEVEN

As if they'd agreed ahead of time, Mary and Henry linked arms and headed toward the next house. When a car door slammed behind them, Mary fought not to turn and look at whoever was there.

"What now?" Henry whispered out of the corner of his mouth as he ambled along.

Mary patted his arm and tried to smile as if she were enjoying a walk along the beach with an old friend. "We keep moving unless anyone says something."

The next house was more of a cottage. It had a Cape Cod look mixed with a modern remodel. It didn't quite fit, yet the small yard that fronted the beach was well maintained, with hints of landscaping that would come to life when the temperatures warmed.

Mary pivoted slightly to see if the driver was watching them. Her breath returned to normal when she saw the person had actually walked toward the beach with a chair and blanket. Maybe someone who wanted to watch the sunset on this chilly evening?

Mary couldn't be sure, so she'd keep an eye on where he sat as she and Henry continued their search.

"Come on, Henry." Mary hurried around the home, which had the slightly abandoned look of a house that had been empty for a while. When she finally found a window with more than a crack between the curtains, she saw a sheet draped over a chair. "No one's living here."

"I agree." Henry cut across the yard toward the next cottage, one that was larger with a single light glowing in an upstairs window, a silhouette of warmth in an otherwise closed-looking place. The sand along the walkway looked as though it had been raked.

"Have you ever raked the sand around your house, Henry?"

He snorted as he kept walking around the house. "No reason to go to that trouble. The wind will just blow it around again."

"That light could be on a timer."

"Sure. I do that when I'm not home."

Mary tried to look in the windows but couldn't see anything useful. The sun was speeding its descent toward the bay. Mary picked up her pace, breaking into a jog as she moved along the front of the house and then toward the next home. This one was large, almost imposing in its Victorian style after the two cottages.

"Come on, come on." Mary hurried up the steps on to the porch. "Where are you, Betty?" She had to be here somewhere. While they'd found the Surf City Snack Shack, there were so many houses to search. She was running out of time to find the right one before the ransom drop.

God, please.

The curtains drawn across the front windows were gauzy. The fading daylight flowed through them, casting spider webs across the room.

"See anything?" Henry moved down the wraparound porch toward another set of windows.

"Not yet."

But there was something about this house. She kept peering through the window, adjusting her angle, looking for just the right perspective. The walls were beige like so many beach homes she'd seen in the pages of magazines. While the outside was a traditional Victorian, the inside had clean, modern lines. Magazines were scattered across a coffee table that was too far away for her to attempt to read the address labels.

Was there anything in the open living room that could be Betty's? Mary squinted, trying to see into deeper reaches of the home.

On the floor by the distressed entertainment center—was that a purse? In the gathering late-afternoon shadows, it was hard to see details, but it looked similar to the one Betty carried. Large enough to hold a billfold, phone, and toiletries, it had a strap adorned with a leather rosette. Betty wasn't the only one to carry a purse of that style, but it kept Mary glued to the window.

She shifted to the next window, hoping to see something different from there.

"Mary, what was in that photo?" Henry called from around the corner of the house.

"A blank wall with a stick of some sort."

"Do you think it could be something to do with sports?"

"I suppose." She reluctantly pulled her face from the window and turned toward him. "What do you see?"

"There's a stick over here. You might want to check."

She walked to Henry's window. "Where?"

"Over there." He pointed toward the corner by a buffet. "See how if Betty stood against the wall by the buffet, we wouldn't see the furniture, but there's a stick leaned against the side?"

Mary looked where he indicated and saw it. "You're right. That looks like a lacrosse stick." She pulled out her phone and dialed Chief McArthur.

He answered immediately this time. "Mary?"

"I think we've found it." She explained quickly about the purse inside that looked like Betty's and the lacrosse stick that could be the wood from the photo. "Can you send someone?"

After a brief pause in which she heard him speak in muffled tones to someone, he responded. "Wadell's already on his way. Tell me exactly where you are."

Mary hurried off the porch to a place where she could read the house number.

"Got it."

Mary glanced around the home. It seemed abandoned. If Betty was in there, she was away from the main floor. And it didn't look like anyone was home. "Do you want me to knock and see if anyone's here?"

"No. Wait until the police arrive. I'll have local police meet Bobby so there won't be any jurisdictional issues." He sighed. "We should receive the final ransom drop instructions anytime. Let Deputy Wadell and the locals handle checking the house. Do you understand, Mary?"

"Understood."

She turned back to the house and hurried up the steps to where Henry waited on the side porch. When she reached him, he put an arm around her. The need to get to Betty, to know for sure if she was inside, burned inside Mary, but she knew the chief was right. The last thing she wanted to do was something rash that would prevent the kidnapper from being fully prosecuted later. She leaned against Henry, felt the comfort of his arms, and watched through the window. Any breath of movement would have her fighting not to barge into the home immediately.

"We're so close, Henry."

She shivered and huddled deeper into her coat. She would not leave until the police arrived and checked the house. Was the heat on inside? She hoped so, because otherwise it must be bitterly cold as the sun set and the temperatures dropped.

A car door slammed just as her phone vibrated. She slipped it out of her pocket and glanced at the display. A text from Chief McArthur. "They have the ransom drop instructions."

Her hands trembled at the thought that Betty would soon return. Either from finding her in this house or from the delivery of the ransom. She refused to consider the alternative, though the way her stomach wanted to fly away, she felt the adrenaline race through her.

This would be over soon. If Deputy Wadell arrived in time and Betty was inside, they could stop the ransom drop and protect Eleanor's money.

The crunching of steps along the gravel path leading to the house reached Mary, and she eased back into Henry. He stilled as if sensing her silent plea that they wait to see who it was. If this was the kidnapper returning, she wanted to know.

She eased around the side of the house to get a look. The last thing she wanted to do was spook whoever it was, but she couldn't let him by if this was the kidnapper and Betty was inside.

The person reached the steps and clomped up them, making a lot of racket for someone as tall and thin as he was. Mary bit back an exclamation when she recognized him. Henry squeezed her arm as if to let her know he recognized the man too.

Connor Hannon reached the top step whistling an off-key tune. He stilled, the tune whining to an abrupt end. He glanced around, and Mary pulled back.

She wasn't quick enough. Connor threw the paper bag he was carrying her direction and took off down the steps.

The sack hit the porch in front of her and exploded. Rice and beef and chicken flew through the air, and a couple of egg rolls landed at her feet.

"Connor, stop!" Mary yelled, but Henry had already taken off after the young man. "Be careful, Henry!"

He didn't acknowledge her as he ran after Connor, arms pumping as he picked up speed. While Henry might be in his early sixties, all his activity on his boats kept him in top condition. Mary held her breath as Henry gained on the scrawny student.

Connor glanced over his shoulder and poured on speed. At that rate, Henry might not catch him. They raced along the beach. Mary wasn't sure where Connor could go. He'd left his car behind, and other than the empty snack shack and surrounding homes, there was nothing in this area.

She pulled her phone out and dialed the chief, hurrying down the steps as she waited for him to pick up. "Come on, pick up."

"Mary? This better be urgent because we have forty-five minutes to drop off."

Connor tripped over something, losing a few seconds that let Henry close the gap again.

"Henry's chasing after a young man. I think he's the kidnapper."

"Where's Bobby?"

"Not here yet."

Chief McArthur muttered something, then said, "Hang on."

A minute later, he was back. "Wadell is within a couple of minutes. Don't do anything crazy. I'm handing you over to the dispatcher because Bobby will need to know where you are."

Mary huffed a reply, as she hurried after the two men. As she watched, Henry took a flying leap and tackled the younger man. Connor hollered and tried to roll Henry off him, but it didn't work.

"Get off me!" Connor swore as he struggled beneath Henry.

"Not until the police arrive, young man." Henry straddled him, both men breathing hard, and then looked up at Mary. "When's the cavalry arrive?"

The dispatcher spoke, and Mary relayed the message. "Bobby's parking near the house. Local police are a couple of minutes behind him."

TWENTY-EIGHT

——◆◆——

Henry crossed his arms and settled more firmly onto Connor. The young man groaned.

"I'm going to sue you for everything you have, Grandpa."

"You are a delusional young man, aren't you, Connor?"

Since Henry had Connor under control, Mary turned back to the house to meet the deputy when he arrived. "I'll send Deputy Wadell your way."

Henry waved her on. "We aren't going anywhere."

When Mary reached the house, Deputy Wadell hurried around the corner of the yard, alert with a hand on his gun.

"Where's Henry?"

"He's down the beach about one hundred feet to the left."

"Don't go anywhere."

Mary nodded as he took off in the direction she'd indicated. She should wait, she knew she should, but as the seconds ticked by, she couldn't ignore the certainty that Betty was inside.

In a few moments, Deputy Wadell was back, a firm hand on Connor as he spoke into the radio on his shoulder. He must have noticed her tension. "We'll wait a minute for the locals to arrive, then get inside, Mary."

"All right." Mary tried to be patient, but she was ready to have her sister back. She turned to Connor, who stood sullenly beside Deputy Wadell, his hands secured in handcuffs. "Why did you do it?"

"I didn't do anything." The kid's snarl seemed to cover something haunted and broken. As she studied him, Mary almost felt sorry for him.

"It's five thirty." Henry's words reminded her of the ransom drop.

"Will they still do the drop?" Connor asked.

Deputy Wadell shook his head. "You've been sloppy about this kidnapping from the beginning, but saying in one second you 'didn't do it' and then asking about the drop the next wasn't your smartest move." He looked at Mary. "Great work, Mary."

She smiled, grateful for so many things. To have found the kidnapper, for one, and that he wasn't anyone she knew and loved.

The local police arrived—two officers who exchanged information with Deputy Wadell. He nodded toward Mary. "We think her sister's inside."

The local officer turned to Connor. "Is she in there?"

Connor now refused to meet their gazes or say a word.

"All right." The officer nodded to his partner. "You stay here with the suspect, and we'll check out the house."

After Connor had been handed off, Henry decided to stay and keep an eye on him. Mary followed Deputy Wadell and the local officer to the door.

The local officer knocked hard. "Open up. Police." He repeated the knocking and the yell, then turned the doorknob.

The latch hitched as if stuck, then eased open without a squeak. The two officers worked their way through the main floor, sweeping the rooms in tandem, as if they'd practiced the process rather than just met minutes earlier.

Mary followed them cautiously. The front room was as stark and crisp as it had looked through the windows. The kitchen sat to the side, connected by a wide doorway, and warm honeyed cabinets lined its walls.

On a slim table against the wall rested a stack of *Cape Cod Living*. The address label on the top issue verified this was Connor's family beach home.

A staircase rose to the right, and Mary took a steadying breath. Chances seemed strong that Betty would be tucked in a room upstairs. The two officers met at the staircase, then eased up the stairs. The silence was eerie and seemed to cloak the house in that stillness one would expect from a boarded-up cottage, not a lived-in house Connor was bringing takeout to.

At the top of the stairs, Mary noted four doors. The local officer tried the first one while Deputy Wadell approached the second.

The first two rooms were both empty. The third door revealed a small bathroom that Deputy Wadell quickly cleared.

The three of them approached the last door. This had to be the one or else Mary had made a terrible mistake.

"Betty, please be here," Mary whispered.

The local officer rapped on the door. "Mrs. Emerson, I'm with the police. Can you hear me? Mrs. Emerson?"

"I'm here! Is Mary with you?"

Tears immediately pooled in Mary's eyes, and through a tight throat, Mary replied, "I'm here, Betty!"

She watched the officer turn the doorknob, but it was stuck. He rattled the door, but it didn't budge. "Mrs. Emerson, did you lock the door? Can you open it?"

"No, he does something to keep it firmly closed. I've tried and tried and can't get out." Betty's voice sounded weary and heavy, as though the pain from her arthritis had flared up over the course of her ordeal.

Mary glanced around the narrow hallway but didn't see anything that could unlock the door. "The door should lock from the inside," she called to Betty.

"I don't see how." Her sister fell silent, the only noise reaching Mary a light thumping as if Betty explored the door again. "I've spent two days trying to find a way to get out. I'm ready to go home."

Deputy Wadell eased Mary to the side. "If we have to take it off the hinges, we will." He pushed on the door and twisted the knob. Nothing. It didn't even budge. "Step back, Betty."

While Deputy Wadell further examined the door, Mary called the chief.

"Mary, we've got a ransom drop to make."

"You don't, Chief. Only one door separates us from Betty, and the local police have the kidnapper."

"That's great news, Mary." The chief's voice was intent, though weary. "If there's a door separating you from Betty, tell Deputy Wadell to kick it down."

She covered the phone and relayed the message to Deputy Wadell. He looked at the local officer, who shrugged. Deputy

Wadell stepped back and threw his shoulder into the door. With one thrust, the door banged open, breaking the frame.

"Thank you for everything you've done to find her, Chief. Deputy Wadell just broke down the door."

"Good. Come by the station as soon as you're back. We'll get your statement down, and you can start putting this behind you."

"All right." Mary hung up and followed Deputy Wadell into the room with a cry of relief. Betty sat on the edge of a wrought-iron twin bed. She'd wrapped a blanket around her shoulders but looked well. Mary hurried to her sister's side and sank onto the bed next to her.

Betty smiled, warmth lighting her face. "I knew you'd find me."

"It took me too long to figure out what you meant by 'hang ten.'"

Betty laughed. "It was an off-the-cuff thought."

"Well, I'm here now, so it worked, just not as quickly as I wanted."

Mary hugged Betty, and as Betty returned the hug, Mary felt the coil of tension inside her release. Tears streamed down her cheeks. She felt Betty's tears as they continued hugging.

Mary sniffed, then squeezed Betty's shoulders again. "Are you okay?"

"I'm a little worse for wear but okay. He basically gave me a little food and ignored me the whole time. I've done nothing but pray."

"Oh, Bets. Let's get you out of here."

"I've never been happier to leave the beach." Betty's smile wobbled for just a moment. She eased to her feet, a tightness communicating how sore and pain-filled her arthritic joints must be. "I'm also ready to get back to our home, our town, and our friends." She wiped the tears from her cheeks.

Betty stumbled, and Mary stepped closer. "Don't rush it, Bets. We've got you, and we're going home."

Betty sagged against her.

Mary met Deputy Wadell's gaze over Betty's head. The young man's eyes were suspiciously misty, but his gaze was pleased. He nodded at Mary with a smile. "Can I help escort you ladies downstairs?"

Mary returned his smile, so grateful this kidnapping had ended so differently from his first. She put an arm around Betty's shoulders. "That would be wonderful."

Betty shook her head. "I've spent the last two days dreaming of the moment I would walk out of this room." She leaned her head on Mary. "I wasn't sure when I would do it, but I always knew you'd be here with me, Mar."

Mary swallowed back her tears. "I'm so glad God protected you, Bets. Let's get you home."

"Home." Betty smiled. "It's a beautiful word."

TWENTY-NINE

After telling her story twice—once to each set of police officers—and listening to Betty's once, Mary was ready to leave. The police knew where to find them, but for now, Mary wanted to get Betty back home to Ivy Bay. Mary had called Eleanor to share the good news. Then she called Pastor Miles and Rebecca, so they could spread the word to their friends. Anyone Pastor Miles and Rebecca missed would find out when Johanna broke the news on the paper's Web site.

Betty was coming home.

Henry stomped up the porch stairs and then inside, his clothes scuffed and dirty from tackling Connor and holding him down in the sand. He'd never looked more rugged and handsome.

Mary hurried to him, and he squeezed her so tightly she squealed. "You did it, Mary girl."

"We did." She placed her hands on his cheeks and smiled. "Thank you."

"I wouldn't have been anywhere else."

Betty cleared her throat, a mischievous glint in her eyes. "Thank you for all you did, Henry. Are you free to chauffeur us back home?"

Henry looked at Deputy Wadell, who nodded. "I'd like nothing better." Henry offered Betty his arm and then assisted her down the stairs.

A minute later, Mary slipped into the backseat next to Betty, grateful Henry had driven it over from the snack shack. The two sat shoulder to shoulder in the small backseat of Henry's vintage car, almost as if the calendar had rolled back to when they were teens. Mary touched Betty's arm, uncertain when she'd let Betty out of her sight again.

As Henry started the car, Deputy Wadell hurried up. "Call the chief first thing tomorrow and come by the station. We'll have your statements ready to sign."

"Thank you, Deputy."

The car trip passed quietly but quickly as they glided toward Ivy Bay in the darkness and finally arrived home. It was a sweet moment when they walked through the front door and Gus meowed a welcome. After they were securely inside, Henry hugged them both and left.

Mary led Betty to her room. "What can I get for you?"

"I'm taking a couple of Tylenol, then soaking in the tub for as long as the water stays warm." Betty smiled, but the same edge of pain tinged it. "I should feel better after that."

Mary nodded, knowing her sister would need more than a bath to get over the traumatic event. But Betty was strong. She *would* recover. "I'll get the tea going."

An hour later, Betty, dressed in flannel pajamas and slippers, settled next to Mary on the couch. Soft music played in the background as they sipped mugs of hot tea.

"Was it terrible?" Mary asked.

Betty shrugged. "Not really." She shook her head. "Well, that's not exactly true. It was terrible to know you'd be worried. And it was horrible to think what Eleanor would be going through." Betty leaned against Mary. "You're both so strong. I just knew I had to be as strong as you while I waited for you to find me."

The phone rang, and Mary retrieved it. "Hello."

"Mary, this is Rebecca." Mary listened as Rebecca asked a series of questions. Rebecca sighed. "I hate to bother you, but they wondered if we could host it here at the bookshop."

"Sure. Just tell them it has to be tomorrow evening."

"I will."

Mary hung up, then picked up her mug again.

"What was that all about?" Betty asked.

"People want to have a party for you."

"Good heavens."

"Let them, Betty. So many people were terribly concerned."

"Okay. It will be good to see everyone."

The next evening, Mary drove Betty to the bookstore. The familiar shops welcomed them. Bailey's Ice Cream, the Black & White Diner across from the Tea Shoppe, Sweet Susan's Bakery, Gems & Antiques, and Meeting House Grocers.

When she parked in front of Mary's Mystery Bookshop, every light in the store was on. As Betty stepped from the car, a flood of their friends rushed from the store. Mary waited until everyone had a chance to greet Betty.

Eleanor led the way, a big smile on her weary face. "Betty, you're back." She wrapped her sister-in-law in a hug, and Mary was pretty sure she was the only one who heard Eleanor whisper, "Don't ever do that again."

Betty rolled her eyes but hugged Eleanor back. "I don't plan on it."

Mary and Eleanor flanked each side of Betty as she walked toward the shop. D.J. approached slowly, as if unsure what kind of response he'd get. Betty quickly embraced him. Watching them, Mary felt certain that D.J. had no idea what his roommate had done.

"Betty, I don't know what happened. I guess Connor was more desperate than I imagined. We all talked about how expensive school is, but his parents have money." He shrugged, hands shoved deep in his pockets. "I don't understand."

"He told the police he heard you say Eleanor was wealthy," Mary said gently, making sure nothing in her tone was accusing.

"Just once, when he asked about my family," D.J. said. "She's an Emerson, so of course she has money."

Once had been enough. Mary had heard Deputy Wadell interview Connor after they found Betty, and her compassion for the troubled young man had only grown. An only child and used to his parents' undivided attention— and generosity—Connor had watched his world turn upside down during his parents' divorce. Suddenly there wasn't enough money to pay for his hefty tuition at MIT, and rather than lower himself to a less prestigious school, Connor had recklessly assumed a couple of "old ladies" would be an easy target. He was young, foolish, spoiled, and entitled, but he was also distraught, lost, and alone. His parents, so mired in their own concerns, seemed to have forgotten they had a son who still needed them. Mary found it easy to forgive him.

Mary spotted Dr. Anderson and headed in his direction. Henry winked at her as she passed him chatting with Pastor Miles. Dr. Anderson brushed his hands across his pants as she approached. "Learn anything interesting while you were here?" she asked.

He shrugged. "I'm not sure. I am grateful you found your sister unharmed. These kinds of things don't always end this well."

"I know." She surveyed the crowd gathered inside the store. "When do you head back to MIT?"

"In a couple of days. I won't be back to Ivy Bay until the semester ends."

"Maybe we'll bump into each other."

He nodded, and she and Betty went inside the shop, where Betty was quickly surrounded by their friends. As Jayne Tucker hugged Betty, Mary was grateful God had brought Betty back home.

Mary stood back and let the crowd love Betty. Mary felt blessed. When she'd come to Ivy Bay to live with Betty after John's death, she hadn't been sure what her life would look like. Now it was a rich tapestry of friends and a community that felt like home. The town she'd summered in growing up had developed into a place she couldn't imagine leaving.

Rebecca stepped next to Mary. "Do you see the ice-cream bar?"

Mary shook her head, then laughed as she saw that the marble-topped counter in her store had been turned into a sundae bar. "Let me guess…"

"Your new flavor. Tess decided this was the perfect way to celebrate Betty's safe return." Rebecca pointed to the coffee area in back. "Sophie provided an assortment of teas, and Susan brought a platter of mini-cupcakes. It's a wonder I didn't eat them all while we were setting up."

Ashley, Rebecca's young daughter, sidled up to Mary, ribbons tied into her pigtails. "Is Betty okay?"

Mary crouched in front of her. "She is."

"I prayed really hard while she was gone."

"Everybody's prayers worked. She's here."

"Maybe she'd like a cupcake." Ashley looked at Betty, who was surrounded by Tricia Miles and several other ladies from church. "If they have their way, she'll never get food. I'd better get her a couple of cupcakes." Ashley marched off, purpose in every line of her body.

Eleanor approached Mary, weariness cloaking her but a smile also peeking out. "Thanks for finding Connor when you did."

"You're welcome."

"My money is back at the bank. Where it belongs. But even more important, Betty's back home where she belongs."

Mary accepted a bowl of ice cream from Paige Bailey. "Thank you for being willing to pay the ransom."

"I love her too, Mary. I may not show it the same way you do, but Betty's an important person in my life." Eleanor turned to walk away, then stopped. "Nice job on the ice cream."

Mary watched carefully as so many of their friends approached Betty. After a while, Betty's smile was slower to appear, and her shoulders began to droop. She still hadn't recovered fully from her ordeal.

Mary turned to Rebecca. "Thanks for organizing this celebration. I think I'd better get Betty home."

"I'm so glad to do it. Don't worry—I'll clean up before I leave."

"We'll get it in the morning." When Mary approached Betty, her sister straightened. "Ready to head home, Betty?"

"Sounds wonderful. Give me a minute to say good-bye?"

Mary nodded and collected their coats before heading toward the door to wait. The bell tinkled as Chief McArthur entered the store, followed by Deputy Wadell and Annaleigh Wadell. Mary felt a pang as she considered all the ways she'd been convinced the deputy was involved.

"Well, Mary, you did it." The chief stopped in front of her, his height towering over her.

"We did it. Thank you."

He dipped his head once, then smiled. "I'm just glad this ended well."

Betty walked up and took her coat and purse from Mary. She smiled as she saw the chief and Deputy Wadell. "Thanks for finding me."

Chief McArthur smiled. "It was a team effort, Betty. Welcome home."

Betty nodded and turned to Mary. "Ready?"

A few minutes later, Mary pulled into their driveway. They were home. As they walked up the slate path, Gus waited, silhouetted in the window. When she opened the door, he walked past Mary to Betty and twined around her legs, purring at full force.

Betty bent over and patted his head. "I don't think I'll ever take for granted how good it is to come home."

It *was* good to be home. But it was better to be home with Betty. Everything felt right and good.

They were home, right where they both belonged.

ABOUT THE AUTHOR

Cara Putman, the award-winning author of nineteen books, graduated high school at sixteen, college at twenty, and completed her law degree at twenty-seven. She is active at her church and a lecturer on business and employment law to graduate students at Purdue University's Krannert School of Management, where she's currently pursuing a master of business administration. Putman also practices law and is a second-generation homeschooling mom. She serves on the executive board of American Christian Fiction Writers (ACFW) and lives with her husband and four children in Indiana. You can connect with her online at www.caraputman.com.

MARY'S ST. PATRICK'S DAY DELIGHT

◆

2 cups heavy whipping cream
1 (14-ounce) can sweetened condensed milk
1 cup milk
1 teaspoon mint extract
½ teaspoon vanilla extract
¼ cup chopped walnuts
¼ cup heavily drained pineapple (small pieces)

Stir heavy cream, sweetened condensed milk, milk, mint extract, vanilla extract, and walnuts in a bowl until evenly mixed.

Pour mixture into an ice-cream maker and freeze according to manufacturer's directions until softly frozen. Transfer ice cream to a lidded container. Stir in pineapple. Cover surface with plastic wrap and seal. For best results, ice cream should ripen in the freezer for at least two hours to overnight.

FROM THE GUIDEPOSTS ARCHIVES

——◆◆◆——

Greater love hath no man than this, that a man lay down his life for his friends. —John 15:13

My sister and I are so different. She is Joan Van Ark, who plays Valene on the long-running TV show *Knots Landing*, and lives in Hollywood where life is full of glitter. I live in Boulder, Colorado, on the same plot of land where we grew up, and my main focus in life is my family. In spite of our differences, we keep in close touch. That's why I wasn't too surprised when she called a couple of weeks ago.

"Carol," she said excitedly, "can you fly to New York on Monday to be on *The Joan Rivers Show* with me? The subject is 'best friends' and I said my sister is my best friend."

I was speechless for a moment, and then filled with reasons why I couldn't go: I didn't have anything to wear; I felt afraid of flying alone; I wouldn't know what to say on such a TV show. But somehow I knew I had to say, "Yes" to being her best friend.

The days whirled by and suddenly I found myself seated in that TV studio next to my sister, who was saying, "We are different—but she is always ready to talk to me, even if I call and wake her up in the middle of the night."

Then it was my turn, and I remembered how my sister dropped what she was doing in California and came to Colorado to be with me when each of our three children was born. *Presto!* The show was over, but I kept thinking about the interview and realized that "being alike" isn't what matters most in close relationships. It's being willing to put the other person's needs ahead of your own. It means giving up sleep. Or time. Or fears.

Jesus, teach me what it means to "lay down my life" for another.
—Carol Kuykendall

A NOTE FROM THE EDITORS